Chili Chili Bang Bang

A Chef-to-Go Mystery

DENISE SWANSON

http://www.DeniseSwanson.com

Chili Chili Bang Bang

ISBN-13: 9798860902121

Chili Chili Bang Bang

From *New York Times* best-selling author Denise Swanson.

Dani Sloan will have to solve the Chili Challenge murder before she or one of her fellow competitors' chances of surviving the contest aren't worth a hill of beans. Once again, it looks like Dani's best-laid plans have been blown up...

* * *

Things in Normalton, Illinois are getting hot, hot, hot. When the small Midwest college town is chosen to host the Route 66 Rally's Chili Challenge, not everyone's excited by the prospect. Campus activists are upset about the environmental impact, the economic inequity, and the consumption of meat.

And when the contestants' ingredients and equipment are peppered with sabotage, it becomes clear that there's someone who's willing to take a life to get their point across, and Dani must not only cook a killer batch of chili, she also has to follow a trail of clues to save the contest, her fellow competitors...

And herself.

Chapter 1

Dani Sloan had put it off as long as she could. Telling herself that she was too busy was all well and good, but it didn't make the situation any better. It was time to accept the consequences and do what had to be done.

She ignored the strident cacophony coming from the second floor. Usually, she'd be up there reminding her lodgers to put on their headphones or earbuds, but she could only handle one problem at a time. Besides, reprimanding her boarders would involve untying the rope, getting down from the ladder, and climbing up the stairs.

The music stopped and she blew out a sigh of relief, but before she could take another breath it started right up again. Letting out a shriek of exasperation she narrowed her eyes and glared at the ceiling.

Evidently, whichever girl was responsible for the concert had decided on another selection, this one even more jarring than the original one. Tippi Epstein was Dani's first guess as to the culprit's identity. She was the most self-centered of the three college coeds who occupied one of the house's suites in exchange for her parents paying rent and Tippi working a certain number of hours a week for Dani's Chef-to-Go business.

Rolling her eyes, Dani continued on her mission. It didn't really matter who was to blame for the noise, she couldn't stop now. Still, as she tightened the knot, her mind reviewed the sign-out board in the kitchen. Who was home?

Starr Fleming was already gone. Although a senior, having switched majors from prelaw to premed, she was playing catch up by taking the first of the required two inorganic chemistry courses. It met at seven a.m., and she didn't dare miss a single lecture if she wanted to pass, so that she could get into the second class next semester.

Starr had left the house at six-thirty, way before they'd finished assembling the day's Lunch-to-Go meals. Her early departure had been the start of Dani's bad day.

The remaining possibility was her youngest resident, Ivy Drake. However, it would be unusual for Ivy to break the rules. Her Uncle Spencer was Dani's boyfriend, as well as head of Normalton University campus security. Poor Ivy didn't even try to get away with much.

A quick glance at her watch and Dani groaned.

Her Lunch-to-Go customers would be arriving any minute. Making sure the rope holding the chandelier up out of the way was tied tightly, she reluctantly climbed down the ladder, almost tripping on the large white dog sprawled on the floor below her. He shot her a goofy grin and darted from the room.

She yelled after him, "You know you aren't allowed in the house by yourself, Khan. Whoever keeps opening the door for you is in deep trouble."

Dani frowned. Had she made a mistake allowing Khan to live with Atti in one of the three apartments that had been recently carved out of the old carriage house? There'd been enough square footage for two nice-sized one-bedroom accommodations; one had been eagerly snapped up as soon as it was finished and the other was waiting for a suitable tenant.

The remaining space had been converted into a tiny studio that Dani had offered to Atti, an eighteen-year-old she'd found living by herself at the homeless camp under the old railroad overpass a couple of blocks from the college's quad. Since the girl had no money, Dani's agreement with her was that she would work twenty hours a week for the Chef-to-Go business and in exchange she would live rent free, have all her meals provided, and receive a small stipend for incidentals.

A series of chimes snapped Dani out of her

revery and sent her running into the kitchen. The first of her Lunch-to-Go customers had arrived and she couldn't afford to disappoint them.

The weekday meals she provided to busy college students, were what brought in the day-to-day cash flow her business needed to succeed. Sure, the huge catering jobs were lucrative, and her personal chef service was doing well, but neither of those provided the steady income of her lunches.

Grabbing her chef's apron, she paused to slip it over her head. Tying it on, she rushed to the pass-through window that she had had installed near the back door and slid it open.

She greeted her first patron by asking, "Healthy or indulgent?"

Dani offered two choices for her takeout meals. Both had an entrée, side, and dessert and were packaged in her signature red-and-white striped paper bags, but one option had less sugar, carbs, and fats than the other.

Business was brisk and it was nearly two o'clock before the last credit card was swiped through the machine attached to the narrow shelf under the window. Dani had just turned on the dishwasher when her cell phone started to play Madonna's "Papa Don't Preach."

Digging it out of her apron pocket, she

answered, "Hello, Dad."

"Are you home?" The voice of Jonas Sloan thundered through the speaker. When she assured him that she was, he said, "I'll be there in a few minutes."

Her father hung up without further explanation or before Dani could tell him it wasn't a good time to come by. She growled in aggravation. They didn't have a drop-in kind of relationship, and as she walked down the hallway toward the foyer, she couldn't imagine what he wanted.

Granted, Dani and her father were doing better. They were keeping in touch, and her dad had been the one to find the construction company that had remodeled the carriage house for her. But years of his neglect and criticism made Dani less than comfortable with the announcement of his abrupt visit.

As she hurried past the vestibule mirror, Dani caught her reflection. With her dark blonde curls in a messy bun and the only paint on her face a tiny smudge of the Agreeable Gray that she was using on her dining room walls, which did nothing for her amber eyes, she looked awful.

Her torn jeans and paint spattered T-shirt didn't help her appearance. But at least the bright red Chef-to-Go apron she wore was clean. Hoping it made her look somewhat professional, she decided to leave it on.

Dani knew it would take too much time to transform herself into a woman who would come anywhere near to meeting her father's high standards. She'd never been able to please him. None of her accomplishments were enough for him—not even graduating summa cum laude—and her less-than-slim figure was a constant disappointment.

In her dad's eyes, Dani didn't come close to her mother's perfection. He didn't understand that living up to the memory of the gorgeous woman he'd loved and lost at such a young age was an impossible goal for his daughter. She just didn't have the raw materials to work with. Her mother's face rivaled any movie star's, and her body could have easily been on the cover of *Vogue*.

The closest Dani had ever come to gaining her father's approval had been when she'd started dating Kipp Newson. Her dad had been so impressed that she was involved with such a handsome, successful doctor that she'd continued to see the scumbag long after she should have come to her senses and broken up with him.

If Ivy hadn't discovered Kipp's second Facebook page showing that he was engaged to another woman, Dani might still be wasting her time with that loser. Thankfully, that wasn't the case, and she was now seeing a wonderful guy who thought she was beautiful.

Keeping that in mind, Dani resolved not to let her father upset her. She turned away from the mirror, stepped toward the door and flung it open.

Her dad was just hurrying up the stairs, and before he reached the porch she asked, "What's up?"

Silence greeted her as he continued his climb, clutching his chest. His gray-blond hair was slicked back and although it was by no means a hot day, sweat glistened on his forehead. The wrinkles around his mouth were etched so deeply they looked painful, and his expression was aggrieved.

Dani held her breath. Was he having a heart attack?

Chapter 2

Seconds later, Jonas rushed into the foyer, waved a flash drive at Dani, and demanded, "Where's your computer?"

He was dressed in sharply creased charcoal-gray slacks, a pale-yellow button-down shirt, and gleaming black loafers. If it weren't for the perspiration dripping down the sides of his face and his rapid breathing, he'd have looked as if he'd just stepped out of his office.

"What's that for?" Dani backed away, refusing to take the tiny silver rectangle.

Jonas ignored her and started down the hallway. "Is your laptop in the kitchen?"

"Yes." Dani hesitated, then shrugged and followed her father.

Jonas marched straight to the device resting on the kitchen counter, and asked, "Where's the USB port?"

"Whoa!" Dani leaped between her father and the laptop, holding up her palm. "Before you stick that thing in my computer, you need to tell me what's on it."

Jonas huffed, "It's easier to show you. Trust me.

This is something you'll want to see."

"O-kay." Dani drew out the word. "You promise it doesn't contain some kind of virus?"

Jonas edged around Dani and ran his finger along the side of the laptop. "Of course not." Finding the little slot, he inserted the flash drive and tapped a few keys. "Look."

He moved out of the way and Dani saw what looked like a memo from her father's employer.

THE ILLINOIS DIVISION OF USA FOODSERVICE EQUIPMENT IS SEEKING A CANDIDATE TO REPRESENT US IN THE UPCOMING ROUTE 66 CHILI CHALLENGE, WHICH WILL TAKE PLACE IN NORMALTON DURING THE ROUTE 66 RALLY. AS OUR PARENT COMPANY HAS DIVISIONS IN EACH OF THE ROUTE 66 STATES, IT HAS DECIDED TO SPONSOR A CHILI CHALLENGE.

THE COMPETITION WILL TAKE PLACE ON THE CAMPUS OF NORMALTON UNIVERSITY NOVEMBER 11-13. EVERY DIVISION WILL SPONSOR ONE CONTESTANT. THE WINNER WILL RECEIVE FIVE THOUSAND DOLLARS, SECOND PLACE WILL RECEIVE ONE THOUSAND, AND THIRD PLACE WILL RECEIVE FIVE HUNDRED.

ALL ENTRANTS MUST BE A RESIDENT OF

THE STATE THEY REPRESENT AND NOT HAVE
WON ANY OTHER COOKING CONTEST.

"Wow!" Dani glanced at her dad. "I take it you
want me to enter?"

"Yes." Jonas pushed Dani down onto a counter
stool. "And you need to do it immediately. The
deadline is noon Pacific time."

"This seems a little last minute." Dani narrowed
her eyes. "Your division should have selected
someone months ago. The event is less than a week
away."

Instead of answering her, Jonas seemed to notice
Dani's appearance for the first time and wrinkled his
nose. "Why do you look like that?"

"I was painting. Remember I told you I was
going to start doing tasting menus once a month for a
select group of clients and needed to redecorate the
dining room in a more modern palette?" Dani
reminded her father, then added, "If you wanted me
all clean and pretty, you should have given me some
warning that you were coming by."

"There was no time." Jonas waved off any
responsibility.

Dani frowned. "Which brings us back to my
original observation. This is clearly last minute.
Why?"

Jonas inched Dani's seat closer to the counter.

"Start filling in the application while I explain."

Dani had a feeling she should resist but complied with her dad's instructions.

Jonas pulled a stool up next to Dani and said, "Now, I want you to promise that you'll think about what I'm going to say before you respond."

"Fine." Dani brought up the application and typed in her name.

"When this first came up last August, my boss asked if any of us had someone we'd like to recommend. At the time, I didn't know you had quit your job and started a cooking business."

Dani paused in entering her address on the form. Her father might not have known about Chef-to-Go, but he had definitely known she liked to cook.

Still, bringing that up would only cause a fight, so she forced herself to say, "Okay. I understand why you wouldn't have suggested me then, but once you became aware of what I was doing, why didn't you mention it?"

"Well." Jonas fiddled with the pen in his shirt pocket. "The thing is, I had already suggested someone, and we were only allowed one submission."

"Oh?" Dani typed her phone number into a box. "Then why am I doing this?"

Jonas stared out the kitchen window. "Because

she withdrew her name."

"Why?" Dani wrinkled her brow.

"She and I had been seeing each other, but she broke up with me." Seemingly determined to get off that subject Jonas quickly added, "She teaches Home Ec at the high school."

"They still have Home Ec?"

"They call it Family and Consumer Sciences now, but cooking is still a part of it."

"Why haven't you ever mentioned her to me?" Dani turned away from the laptop.

Jonas plucked a paper napkin from the holder and started tearing off tiny pieces. "Because I didn't want you to think that I was betraying your mother. I still love your mom—what Beverly and I had was more about companionship than romance."

Dani shook her head. "Mom's been dead for years. I'd have been happy you found someone. I would never be upset that you were finding some happiness."

"Well, it's over.

"I'm sorry to hear that. What happened?"

"Who knows?" Jonas threw up his arms. "Anyway, you're a better cook than she is."

Dani blew out a breath. "And above all, you want to back a winner."

"No! Well, yes." Jonas shoulders sagged. "But

what I really want is for us to be more like a regular father and daughter and for everyone to see how wonderful your food is."

Dani was touched. Oh, she didn't entirely believe him, but for her dad, this was huge progress.

"Okay." She turned back to her laptop and resumed typing. "But I want to hear more about what happened with Beverly."

Jonas grumbled. "I'll tell you later, just concentrate on what you're doing."

"You know, I might not get chosen."

"Believe me, you're a shoo-in." Jonas smiled like he'd just opened a longed-for Christmas gift. "The only other applicant is my boss's teenage daughter whose idea of cooking is burning a frozen pizza."

Dani continued typing, but said, "Maybe he'll want his daughter anyway."

"No." Jonas shook his head. "Trey only made her apply once Beverly dropped out."

"I get to keep the cash if I win, right?"

"Absolutely." Jonas patted her awkwardly on the shoulder. "I'd love to see you get it."

Once Dani finished the application and clicked SEND, Jonas immediately grabbed the thumb drive, pocketed it, and said, "I need to get back to work."

"Sure." Dani nodded and walked with her father down the hall. Before they reached the door, a thought that had been nagging at her subconscious finally surfaced.

She stopped and turned to face him. "How do you know I'm a decent cook? All you've tasted is my baking."

Jonas opened his mouth, but nothing came out.

"You've never eaten one of my meals, have you?"

Jonas studied his fingernails intently.

"Have you?"

"I may have sent a friend's son to buy one of your Lunch-to-Go meals."

"I see." Dani had to bite her lip to keep from giggling as she imagined her father hiding behind a tree waiting for his connection to deliver the goods.

"And I may have crashed a few of the events you catered."

Dani tsked. "Why didn't you just ask me to come to dinner?"

"You might have said no."

Chapter 3

It was November 10, and Dani had just finished meeting with a client finalizing the details for a huge Christmas party the man was throwing for his employees and their families. Now she sat in her empty kitchen sipping a cup of coffee and nibbling on a sweet potato oatmeal muffin left over from her boarders' breakfast.

Being the Thursday before a three-day weekend, many of the Normalton University students had headed home early, and since Dani's Lunch-to-Go sales would be minimal, she'd decided not to bother offering her meals that day.

This had freed her morning for the catering consultation and left the afternoon and evening to work on her chili recipe. And she needed all the time she could get.

In all the rush and excitement of her father's visit, Dani had forgotten that she'd never made a pot of chili in her life. She'd let herself get carried away by the thought of her father's admiration and the cash price. Now she had to face the consequences.

Her reputation was on the line. If she didn't do well in the contest, prospective clients wouldn't

consider her for jobs. And her current patrons may
have second thoughts as well.

Dani's business was only eighteen months old,
and word-of-mouth could either make or break it.
Before agreeing to enter, she should have asked the
identities of the judges. But she hadn't, and it turned
out that one of them was a highly respected member
of Normalton's foodie community.

Which brought Dani back to the question of why
in the world had she jumped into this thing so
recklessly? She felt like slapping herself. She had to
stop trying to gain her father's approval at any cost.

Frowning, she flipped open her notebook and
stared at the pale green paper. The carefully
handwritten recipe with its multitude of crossed-out
and added ingredients mocked her.

Maybe she wasn't the chef she thought she was.
This might be the time her lack of culinary school
training bit her in the butt.

What in heaven's name was she doing wrong?
She'd been practicing this recipe every day since her
father's visit and no matter what she tweaked, it still
tasted like something she'd poured out of a can.

Poor Spencer had dutifully eaten all of Dani's
attempts, and gamely lied, claiming to taste
improvement each time. The girls, however, had been
less careful of her feelings. Last night, Tippi had even

poured her bowl into the trash and ordered pizza.

She wished her friend Gray Christensen was available. But while Gray was an accomplished cook with an amazing palate, he was a police officer by trade, and he was out of town taking a Law Enforcement Executive Development seminar at Quantico.

With the contest starting tomorrow, Dani could only squeeze in two or three more practice pots of chili before she had to stop in order to have time to shop for whatever she might need for the next day. Depending on how the recipe ended up, she might have to go to several specialty stores to get her ingredients and they closed earlier than the large supermarkets.

Okay, she didn't want to think about what would happen if she couldn't figure out the problem with her recipe. Instead, she'd concentrate on how excited everyone in town had been about the Chili Challenge.

Luckily, being a college town, there were plenty of accommodations at the NU's union guest rooms for the contestants, officials, contest staff members, and various media people covering the two-day extravaganza. They were also using several other areas of NU's union for most of the other activities.

The contest's opening ceremony would be in the

south lounge and courtyard on the ground level. Weather permitting, the cooking would take place on the patio, with the second-floor ballroom being the backup plan.

Dani tapped her notebook against her chin, trying to think of what item she should add, subtract, or substitute in her recipe. Maybe she should try it with ground pork instead of ground beef.

As she dug through her refrigerator for the pork shoulder she'd bought the other day, attached the grinder to the countertop, and began to process the meat, she wondered about the other contestants. In addition to Illinois, they were coming from Missouri, Kansas, Oklahoma, Texas, New Mexico, Arizona, and California.

Dani finished grinding and took out a large skillet. Putting it on the burner, she adjusted the flame and went in search of a bottle of peanut oil.

Once the oil was in the pan and heated, she added the ground pork. As it browned, she brightened. While she may not have the best recipe, at least she had the hometown advantage.

Several hours passed, and when she tasted the new batch, she was pleased to discover that the pork had definitely helped the flavor, but there was still something missing. Just as she was starting another pot of chili, her cell phone began playing the theme song from *Law and Order*. When she dug it out of her apron and swiped it, she saw that it was a text from Spencer begging off from dinner.

She wasn't surprised. The poor man would probably never look at a bowl of chili the same again.

It took two more recipe tweaks, including another protein change, before she was satisfied her chili no longer tasted bland or ordinary. Not surprisingly, her boarders decided to go out for supper, but she was too tired to join them.

Instead, she wearily climbed to the third floor, took a quick shower, and fell into bed. Her last thought before dozing off was that unlike a couple of her previous big events where people had died, the worst that could happen with a bowl of chili was heartburn.

Chapter 4

"Son of a—!" Chief of Campus Security Spencer Drake cut himself off.

He slammed down the receiver and glared at the telephone on his desk.

Evidently, the Route 66 Rally events taking place over the next several days were causing a stink among several of the student activist associations.

The Environmental Coalition was unhappy that the Route 66 Rally was glorifying the use of gas-guzzling cars. The Social and Economic Realities Foundation felt that any activities hosted on the campus should be available at no cost to students. The Animal Rights supporters were against any meat being sold or consumed. And the Peace and Love Network were against anything that encouraged competition versus cooperation.

His boss, Dr. Kayley, the university vice-president in charge of safety and security, wanted him to meet with their leaders at six that evening.

It looked like he would be working overtime and probably wouldn't make it over to Dani's in time for dinner.

A second later, he chuckled and shrugged.

Considering supper would probably be her latest experimental recipe for the contest, maybe that was for the best. He'd miss seeing her, but a nice burger and fries would be a relief from the unending bowls of chili he'd consumed the past week.

Thinking about the best way to approach the activists' demands, Spencer walked out of his office and into the conference room. He erased the whiteboard at the front and carefully divided it into four sections — one for each group.

His plan was to have the group representative list their objections. He would then try to dissuade them from calling their members to action by suggesting alternatives and offering various incentives.

However, he wasn't optimistic that he could stop any of them from protesting. The best he could hope for was to contain the demonstrations to areas where his security staff could keep both sides safe from each other.

Blowing out an exasperated breath, Spencer returned to his office to make a list of what he was authorized to offer the groups. He didn't have a lot to bargain with, and after half an hour he threw down his pen.

Spencer pushed back his chair, rose, and checked that he had a portable radio attached to his belt. Then turning off the lights, he stepped into the hallway and locked the door behind him. Since he was stuck working, he needed to go pick up some food before time ticked by and he ended up *hangry*.

As he ran down the stairs, Spencer grabbed his cell from his shirt pocket and sent Dani a text telling her he wouldn't be over. He assured her that he'd see her tomorrow and could only hope that she wouldn't think he was deliberately ducking out of dinner because of her chili.

Frowning, Spencer strode through the lobby. A few steps from the exit, he turned around and made his way to the dispatcher's cubicle. When he got there, he stopped to stare out of the rain-streaked glass. His office was windowless, and he was momentarily surprised by the intensity of the howling gusts and flashing lightning. He'd known that a storm was predicted for later in the evening, but apparently it had arrived early.

Carly paused with one arm in her coat and asked, "Did you need something, sir?"

The daytime dispatcher was a recent addition to his staff and Spencer was still debating whether the position was worth the cost to his budget. They needed someone to answer phones and relay messages, but he wasn't sure if there was enough work to justify her salary. She seemed to spend more time studying than doing her job.

"Just wanted to check in before I left the building. Anything I should know?"

Carly finished putting on her jacket and shook her head. "It's been really quiet today. Probably because of the weather."

"Yeah." Spencer glanced at the downpour.

She smacked her forehead with her palm. "Oh, I almost forgot. The new guy keeps forgetting to let me know when he goes off duty for his breaks."

Spencer frowned. "I'll talk to him about it."

Last week, he'd finally hired a security officer to replace a retiree. Warren Douglas had come highly recommended from the hospital he'd last worked at, and Spencer had been happy to find someone with experience dealing with a vulnerable population. He hoped that Douglas wouldn't be a problem.

Adding a chat with his newest employee to his mental to-do list, Spencer turned his attention to Carly and asked, "Do you need a ride home?"

"Thanks, but my boyfriend is picking me up."

"Okay." Spencer nodded. "See you on Monday."

Carly mumbled something and dashed out the door. Clearly, she was in a hurry to get out of there.

Spencer started to follow her, but halted when the phone rang. With Carly gone, his security staff out patrolling, and the evening dispatcher not here yet, the call would go to an answering service. Which would then be forwarded to Spencer's cell.

Might as well cut out the middleman.

He scooped up the receiver and said, "Campus security."

"My laptop was stolen."

After getting the caller's name and location Spencer asked, "When did it happen?"

"Just now. My dad came into my dorm room and just took it."

Spencer scratched his head. "Your father stole your laptop? Why would he do that?"

"Well. Uh. He sort of owns it, but I need it for class."

"Campus security does not get involved in family disputes." Spencer said goodbye and disconnected.

After grabbing a burger and fries from Meatheads, he returned to the security building and spent the rest of the time before the scheduled meeting in the conference room researching the groups and their leaders. As he enjoyed the juicy burger and crispy fries, he felt a little guilty knowing Dani and his niece were probably eating another bowl of experimental chili.

At five fifty-five there was a knock. He rose to answer it, but before he could do so, the door crashed open clipping him on the side of the head. A woman stood just beyond the threshold. She had her hands on her hips and glared at him.

Without any preamble, she snapped, "That idiot downstairs said the elevator's broken. What if I'd been mobility-impaired?"

"We would have moved the meeting to the ground floor." Spencer forced a smile and held out his hand. "I'm Chief Drake, head of security, and you are?"

Ignoring his outstretch palm, she said, "Charity Greathouse. I represent the Social and Economic Realities Foundation."

"Please come in and take a seat. As soon as the others get here, we'll begin."

Charity appeared to be in her early twenties. Her brown hair was cut short on the sides with long bangs swept to the side and tucked behind her ear.

Heavy dark eyebrows formed a disapproving line across her forehead. "If they aren't prompt, I don't think it's fair of you to waste my time."

"How about we give them a few minutes." Spencer kept his fake smile in place. "As you said, the elevator is out."

Charity selected a chair and sat down. "Fine."

A few seconds later, three others trooped into the conference room. They all seemed slightly out of breath. Evidently, they weren't used to having to climb stairs.

A brawny young man with bright red hair introduced himself as Hamilton Butcher from the Animal Rights group. Spencer had to hide his grin when he heard the guy's name.

Next was Misty Salvador, head of the Environmental Coalition, and bringing up the rear was Quest Lightfoot organizer for the Peace and Love Network.

"I'd like to start with your organizations' primary objections to the Route 66 Rally." Spencer waved to the white board. "If each of you could sum it up for me...?"

"It's elitist. There is no consideration for students without disposable income," Charity huffed.

As Spencer printed "lack of accommodation for those without funds" on the board, Quest twisted his long black hair and finally said, "It's all about trying to win instead of working together. That leads to conflict."

Spencer wrote "competition" in his group's column, and then after Misty spoke, he added "pollution" under the Environmental Coalition's list.

Hamilton crossed his arms. "It's a glorification of animal exploitation."

Spencer dutifully added that sentiment to the

whiteboard.

After an hour Misty had agreed that if the vintage car parade was kept off the campus, the Environmental Coalition wouldn't stage a protest. And Charity had negotiated for fifty free passes to the various events with the understanding that her group would bestow them on whomever they deemed neediest. Sadly, there was little Spencer could offer either Quest or Hamilton. They couldn't make either the Chili Challenge or the Rally noncompetitive, and the best he could do for the Animal Rights people was to promise there would be at least one vegan and/or vegetarian dish available on the various menus.

Neither of the young men were pleased and threatened to organize civil actions.

As Spencer showed Quest out the door, Quest said, "My high school did away with having winners or losers. Why can't the university?"

"Because that bears no resemblance to real life." Spencer was hanging onto his temper by a thread. "When you're an adult, you don't get as many tries as you need to get things right. Life is not divided into semesters. You don't get summers off, and very few employers are interested in helping you find yourself. They expect you to do that on your own time."

Quest pouted. "You'll be sorry you weren't more accommodating — my people can make your life hell."

"That's not very peaceful or loving, is it?" Spencer muttered.

Hamilton was the last to leave and although he didn't say anything, if looks could kill, Spencer would have been mortally wounded.

Chapter 5

Dani fidgeted, trying to keep her balance on the wire-mesh stool that was her assigned seat at the Chili Challenge opening ceremony. She wasn't sure why the university had purchased these torture devices, but they were not designed for comfort or long speeches.

She was afraid she was going to tip over any second and, like a line of dominoes, take her fellow contestants with her. The eight of them were in a jam-packed row behind Wallace Zorillo, the president of USA Foodservice Equipment.

Perhaps it was because she was local, or her habit of being early, but Dani had been the first to arrive. After she was checked off on the list, she was given a black apron with her name and two chilis in the form of an X embroidered across the chest. Underneath were the words: CHILI COOK-OFF CONTESTANT.

Apparently, they wanted their competitors to be easily identified. Maybe the officials were afraid that otherwise they'd get lost in the crowd.

Dani had also received a tote bag full of kitchen hand tools—all products of USE and its subsidiaries — then had her picture taken with Mr. Zorillo. Once that was accomplished, she'd verified her recipe, handed over her ingredients, and was shown to her chair.

Moments later, the other contestants had begun trickling in. Now, with everyone in their seats and as the scheduled time came and went, Dani wondered why Mr. Zorillo didn't start his welcome speech.

The woman on Dani's right was chatting with the person on the other side of her and the man sitting to Dani's left had been on his cell phone since he arrived. As far as she could tell, he was a criminal defense attorney trying to keep his client from doing something stupid.

Dani yawned. It wasn't that she was bored, although she was, it was that she had slept so poorly. She'd had nightmares about monster-size shakers of salt chasing her around a firepit.

Maybe she should go save Spencer. He'd come in ten minutes ago. His handsome face and muscular physique had caused a stir, and he was now surrounded by a group of female journalists vying for his attention.

Shaking her head, Dani decided not to interfere. She didn't want to look like a jealous girlfriend, and the smitten reporters might retaliate by writing something bad about her cooking or her business.

Dani gazed around the patio and counted her blessings that it was a mild fall day. The temperature of an Illinois autumn could range anywhere from thirty to seventy degrees. They were lucky it was a pleasant sixty-five.

Blowing out a fed-up sigh, Dani scrutinized the people milling about. They had been instructed to arrive at 10 a.m., and it was now closer to eleven. The contestants were all there, so who was missing?

Dani wrinkled her nose. Someone nearby was burning leaves. Probably the university's landscaping department. This time of year, it was an uphill struggle to keep the school's lawn pristine. In a battle between the yard crew and the trees, the maples usually won.

Scanning the audience, it was clear everyone was beginning to get impatient. Some wiggled in their seats, others tapped their feet, and a few muttered about "not having all day."

Dani hoped that one of the more vocal spectators would do something. Normally, she would be leading the charge, but she was representing her father and she'd vowed not to do anything to embarrass him.

To amuse herself, Dani turned her attention to the other contestants, trying to guess their day jobs. A man a few years older than Dani sat on the end. He was attractive in a geeky nerdy way, and she immediately put him down as an engineer. Small, wire-rimmed glasses were perched on his nose, and he was studying a recipe card. JM was embroidered on the bib of his official apron.

Next to him was a guy who appeared to be dozing. He was muscular and wore jeans, a plaid shirt, and work boots. Dani pegged him as someone who worked construction or maybe for the utilities.

Dani's attention turned to the women chatting with each other. One had on dark jeans, a black long-sleeved T-shirt, and a pink puffer vest. She was holding her apron and her name wasn't visible.

The woman next to her was similarly attired, but with a blue hoodie. They both had ponytails and ballcaps.

These two were tough to figure out, but Dani guessed that they were either fitness instructors or stay-at-home moms.

On the other side of them was a guy who had to weigh at least three hundred pounds, and it all looked like solid muscle. His long hair was pulled back and fastened at the back of his neck with a piece of leather cord. He wore jeans, a T-shirt with the words The BIG CHILI, and a denim vest. His apron read ELVIS.

Oh. Oh. He was definitely someone to watch out for. Dani wasn't sure what Elvis's profession might be, but she'd bet it was something in the culinary field.

The last contestant's occupation was easy. Her apron had Dr. Jade Lawrence embroidered on it. She was dressed to kill in a tight red wrap dress with sky-high heels and had long scarlet fingernails.

Dani was studying the doctor—her head seemed too large for such a tiny body—when a handsome man swept onto the patio. He was issuing orders to the young woman trailing behind him. "Darling, please don't forget to call my producer. We'll have to put off shooting a few days. My hair is impossible, and Kiyah isn't available until next week." Without waiting for a reply, he went on, "Oh, and I forgot to pick up my new Brioni leather jacket. I'll need it for the judging tomorrow, so call my stylist and have her put it on a plane ASAP."

The man paused to take a breath, and the young woman said, "Yes, sir."

Dani squinted at the guy. He looked familiar. His blond hair was styled in a quiff and his striking blue eyes tickled her memory. It was hard to tell the guy's age—there were slight creases around his eyes, but such extremely fair skin wrinkled easily. He was probably somewhere in his fifties.

What in the world was this Hollywood type doing at a fairly small-time cooking contest? He had to have owed someone a favor.

Chapter 6

Dani was thinking about how bland most of her attempts to make chili had been and what she needed to do to make sure her contest entry didn't suffer the same fate, when the TV personality's posh British accent penetrated her thoughts.

She glanced up and saw that the man was now seated with the other two judges. He was holding a small, leather notebook in his right hand and a sleek black pen in his left. His assistant stood slightly behind him, nodding as he read off items.

The guy's identity finally dawned on Dani. She and Ivy watched his show all the time! He was Hugh Granville, the star of *Carnivore*, a vastly popular television program where cooks competed to come up with the most extreme meat-centric dishes. Their prize was the funds to start up a restaurant, after which they had a year to make it profitable or the backing would be withdrawn.

"And, Amelia," Hugh said, "do tell my wife to make sure Winston gets to the dog park every day. I do not want to find any of his little surprises in my shoes when I get home."

Dani sucked in an audible breath and frowned.

Being a fan of *Carnivore*, she'd had a bit of a crush on him, but his behavior here was rapidly erasing it.

Hugh's gaze fastened on Dani. He glared, then turned back to Amelia and raised his voice. "We seem to have a Nosy Boots eavesdropping on our discussion. Please go over and tell her to mind her own bloody business."

"Sir." Amelia smoothed her dark chin-length bob. "I'm certain no one cares what we're saying."

Hugh ignored her, rose to his feet, and stalked over to Dani. "You there, this is a private conversation. Please do me the ultimate kindness and mind your own business."

"We are outdoors on a stage." Dani was now completely annoyed. "Since everyone but you was on time, the patio is packed, and your voice carries. There is no one in the vicinity who hasn't heard you."

Suddenly, Dani felt someone behind her and looked over her shoulder at Spencer's angry scowl.

He growled, "Is this man bothering you?"

Dani, not breaking eye contact with Hugh, thankful the entries were judged blind, said, "It's fine. Hugh and I were just discussing his reality versus everyone else's."

Spencer shot a pointed look at Hugh, then squeezed Dani's shoulder and walked a few feet away.

Before Hugh could react, Mr. Zorillo tapped the microphone and cleared his throat. He was in his late fifties with short gray hair and steel-blue eyes. He wore a charcoal suit, white shirt, and red patterned tie.

Gesturing to the contestants, he said, "Ladies and gentlemen, it is my pleasure to welcome you to the Route 66 Chili Challenge." He waited for the applause to die down, then continued, "My name is Wallace Zorillo and I'm the president of USA Foodservice Equipment or UFE for short."

When the clapping ceased, Wallace said, "And our hometown judge is Latoya Lin, food editor for *The Normalton Post*."

Dani cringed. While Latoya Lin looked like everyone's favorite grandmother, wearing a floral dress and with a halo of short gray curls that surrounded her round face, she was a brutal critic. Once again, Dani was thankful for the blind judging.

The woman's chubby cheeks and dazzling smile might fool the other contestants, but Dani had read her column for years. She'd hoped to be mentioned in Lin's "Luscious Likes" someday, but not cooking a dish that she might not have truly perfected.

What if Latoya hated her chili and found out it was Dani's? Her business would be ruined. No one would hire her as either a personal chef or a caterer for their big events.

"Our second judge," Wallace said, interrupting Dani's thoughts, "is Mick Owen, bestselling author of *Hot Hot Kitchen*."

The author seemed like a guy who would be right at home behind a grill or smoker. His denim shirt and jeans were well worn and the salt-and-pepper stubble on his chin was probably a permanent feature.

"And our last judge needs no introduction. Please give the star of *Carnivore*, Hugh Granville, a big Normalton welcome."

The TV personality stood a little apart from his fellow judges, his blue eyes shooting sparks of disdain. Something about him reminded Dani of her ex-boyfriend, Kipp. It wasn't his appearance so much as the condescension radiating from his every pore.

After the judges waved to the audience, Wallace turned to the row of contestants. "Now let's meet the competitors. First, Tory Mays, owner of the yoga studio One Octave Higher from California."

Dani smiled. She'd been right. The woman was a fitness instructor.

Wallace continued down the line. "Jill VanAsden from Kansas is a stay-at-home mom who coaches her daughter's soccer team.

Wow! So far, Dani was two for two.

"Next, from New Mexico, we have Dr. Jade Lawrence, a nutritionist and life coach."

Dani's brows met over her nose. Could she count that as a point? The woman was a doctor, just not a medical one.

Elvis Larson, who was a grill master from Missouri, JM Richey, a computer engineer from Texas, and Ruben Caballero, a contractor from Arizona were presented next, then Dani.

Milton McBeal, the lawyer representing Oklahoma was the last contestant to be introduced. After the applause died down Wallace said, "Now, I'd like to tell you all a little about US Foodservice Equipment."

* * *

What seemed like hours later, Wallace finally finished the lengthy description of his company, which had included the history of the business and a detailed description of every subsidiary and every product that division sold.

As soon as he moved away from the podium, Chancellor Verona stepped up. Dani cringed. The head of the university was less than five feet tall and probably didn't weight a hundred pounds, but the woman never met a microphone she didn't like.

With her short gray hair, square jaw, and light blue eyes, she looked a lot like Dame Judith Dench.

Sadly, she didn't have the actress's ability to enthrall a crowd.

While the chancellor started, as expected, by welcoming everyone to the university, Dani's stomach growled. She'd skipped breakfast and it was already past eleven.

She had no hope of food until after the media Q&A, and she wondered if she could surreptitiously slip a package of peanut butter crackers from her purse and eat a few. She didn't want to be known as the chef who fainted from hunger during a cooking contest.

Dani was fingering the crackers' cellophane when the chancellor began her closing remarks. "While we are happy to host this Chili Challenge, I do ask that you all respect that this is an institute of learning and behave accordingly."

The chancellor moved away from the podium and the crowd clapped politely. Wallace immediately stood and opened the floor to the media.

Dani wasn't at all surprised that the majority of the questions were directed at Hugh Granville. What did shock her was his hostile answers.

Dani gaze swept the patio. Where was Granville's assistant? Earlier, it had been clear that one of Amelia's jobs was to keep the television chef from alienating the people around him.

There was no sign of the young woman, and Dani's attention returned to the celebrity judge.

"I like long walks," the man said, responding to a question about his interests. "Particularly when they are taken by people who annoy me. Would you like to take a stroll?"

The audience tittered nervously until a brave soul asked, "What's your number one tip to home cooks?"

"Don't fry bacon in the nude." Hugh smirked.

Dani frowned, clearly some individuals were not meant to be in the limelight without a censor present. They reacted to fame the same way a werewolf reacted to a full moon. The transformation wasn't pretty, and the aftermath was even worse.

Just when she was sure no one else would dare to speak up, a young woman asked, "Why don't you have any restaurants in the Midwest?"

"Because you people think the four food groups are beer, cheese in a can, fried potatoes, and Jell-O salad with marshmallows."

The audience gasped and Wallace swooped in, plucked the microphone from Granville's hand, and announced, "We're all out of time for questions."

Before he could herd the celebrity chef off the stage, Dani's friend and latest renter, Frannie Ryan, reporter for the Normalton newspaper, shouted,

"Why did you agree to be a part of the Chili Challenge, Mr. Granville?"

The TV star rolled his eyes and said, "My agent made me."

Frannie's expression turned predatory. "Why is that?"

Amelia suddenly appeared, leaped forward, and not so subtly shoved her boss behind her. "You all know Chef Granville's wicked sense of humor." Amelia elbowed the celebrity who produced an obligatory smile. "What Chef meant to say was that he was thrilled when his agent offered him this opportunity to meet more of his fans in the Midwest." The audience clapped, and she wrapped it up with, "We hope to see many of you at his book signing tomorrow."

Amelia shot a sideways look of warning to Granville, who had his mouth open but slowly closed it without speaking.

Dani stared at the pair. She'd been right. Amelia wasn't so much the star's assistant as his keeper.

A few seconds later, the contestants were dismissed. Dani took advantage of her knowledge of the university union's layout and headed straight for the nearest restroom.

Dashing inside, she took the first stall, locked the door, and was unzipping her pants when she heard others entering the bathroom.

An angry voice ricocheted off the tile walls. "Listen up, babycakes. Granville is mine. I have too much riding on this for you to try to sway him to vote for your chili."

"Well, aren't you just two scoops of whiny and a bowl full of bitchy?" This voice was mild, but Dani could detect an edge to it. "All I did was say hi to the man, so don't infer that if I win, it's for anything other than the merit of my chili."

"Right. I looked you up. You have no cooking cred whatsoever."

"If I cover you with Preparation H, would you shrink down and become less irritating?"

There were two stall door slams and Dani hurried to get out of there. She quickly washed her hands. But before she could exit the restroom, Jill VanAsden and Tory Mays emerged from their stalls.

Both women stared daggers at Dani as she left.

Chapter 7

Dani frowned as she drove in the procession of vehicles traveling the few miles between the university and the Apple of Eden Café where the contest luncheon was being held. After using the restroom, she hadn't been able to find Spencer, and she wondered where he had gone. He had been invited to the meal and she had been going to suggest they ride together.

She shrugged. He probably had to handle something on campus, and she'd see him there.

Looking around, she noticed that her van with the Chef-to-Go logo on the sides stood out among the nondescript rental cars driven by most of the contestants and judges. That is, except for the imposing black Escalade right behind her.

Hugh Granville was at the wheel, and he was clinging to her bumper like overcooked pasta in the bottom of a pan. What was his problem?

Dani could see his scowling face in her rearview mirror and she chuckled. You would think that living in California, the television star would be used to gridlock.

In contrast, his assistant Amelia's expression was

serene as she talked on her phone. She occasionally patted her boss's arm, but remained Zen-like when he glared at her.

As far as Dani could tell, Amelia was either the calmest person on earth or popping Xanax at an alarming rate.

Dani twisted the knob on the radio until she found the weather. According to the local meteorologist, Normalton was supposed to enjoy clear skies and temperatures in the seventies for the next couple of days.

Staring out the windshield, Dani wasn't sure if she was happy or sad about the prediction. It would be nice for the organizers to have the contestants cooking outside where they'd be more accessible to the Route 66 Rally attendees, but it would be a heck of a lot easier on the chefs to use a regular stove versus one hooked up to a propane tank.

Dani braked at a stoplight and her thoughts wandered back to the acrimonious conversation she had overheard in the restroom. She hoped that kind of attitude wouldn't be prevalent among all the contestants. She hated poor sportsmanlike behavior, and if everyone was bickering, she might get so rattled she'd do something that ruined her recipe.

A few minutes later, Dani made it through the light and turned right into the restaurant's lot. At first glance it was full, and she wondered where else she could park.

Her gaze swept the double rows. All were solidly packed.

She looked down at her sensible black pumps and smiled. If she had to walk, at least she wouldn't break her ankle doing so.

Dani eased the van forward, hoping against hope there was a spot she'd missed seeing. Suddenly, she saw a pickup in the next row backing out. She was just making the turn when a car squeezed around her and zoomed for the vacancy.

"Oh, hell no," Dani muttered and used the size of her van to prevent the other vehicle from stealing her spot.

She whipped into the space and triumphantly shut off the motor. Hopping out, she grabbed her purse, then quickly walked to the restaurant's entrance. Dani was a little afraid that the frustrated driver would run her over, but the woman only revved her engine.

* * *

The population of Normalton might be over fifty thousand, but it was still just a small college town at heart and its residents tended to support any activities associated with the university. Which might be why the Apple of Eden Café was so crowded.

In addition to the contestants, judges, and contest officials, it looked to Dani as if a lot of the people who had attended the welcome ceremony had decided to lunch at the official challenge restaurant. The tables were full, and the noise level was deafening.

The only way Dani could get to her chair was by edging sideways and holding her purse above her head. Once seated, she noticed that most of the other diners were staring at the contestants and judges.

The contestants were scattered among three tables, each hosted by a judge and a contest official. Dani's assigned place was with Elvis, Hugh Granville, Amelia, and Wallace Zorillo. She wondered if it was luck of the draw, or if her father had pulled some strings with his boss's boss to get her preferential seating.

Their lunch orders had been taken that morning, and the food began to arrive as soon as they were all present. It smelled wonderful and Dani reached for her patty melt as soon as everyone was served.

She had just bitten into her sandwich when Wallace turned to her and asked, "So, you have a catering company in Normalton?"

Dani hastily chewed and swallowed. "My business does include a catering arm, but I also do personal chef gigs and have Lunch-to-Go service for the college kids."

Wallace looked amused. "Right. Your father did mention that. He's very proud of you."

"Really?" Dani blurted out before she could stop herself.

Amelia gave Dani a sympathetic look, then said, "This is my first time in the Midwest. I just can't get over all the space."

"Miles and miles of miles and miles." Hugh sneered, cutting a piece of his teriyaki salmon and forking it into his mouth.

"Which is just how we like it." Dani took a sip of her Diet Coke.

Elvis discarded a sparerib bone, licked the barbecue sauce from his fingers, and drawled, "We Midwesterners hide all the good stuff so the people on the coasts stay where they belong. Look what happened to poor Idaho when the Californians started moving in."

Hugh's face reddened and Wallace quickly asked, "What made you decide to enter, Elvis?"

"I didn't." His smile was roguish. "My friend works for your company and loves my Bacon Bison Beer Chili, so she signed me up."

Dani frowned. So much for having the entries judged blind.

"That sounds intriguing." Amelia touched

Elvis's arm. "I can't wait to try it."

"It's a combination of my Choctaw grandmother's recipe and my German grandfather's home-brewed beer." Elvis grinned. "I came up with it when I smoked too much weed one weekend."

Hugh rolled his eyes. "That's not a recipe, that's the munchies."

Wallace frowned, then quickly said, "I know your father enticed you into entering, Dani. What gourmet treat will you concoct for us?"

"Smoky Peanut Butter Chili," Dani answered, resigned to the fact that judging wouldn't be as anonymous as she'd hoped.

"Now that might be interesting." Hugh leaned forward. "What type of wood do you use in your smoking gun?"

"Apple."

"A safe choice. Have you thought of trying mesquite?"

Dani shook her head. "I hadn't, but I'll keep it in mind for next time."

"Its earthiness is a nice contrast." Hugh handed the waitress his half-eaten plate and ordered key lime pie for dessert. "But you have to be careful, or it takes over."

Dani shook her head at the waitress's offer of dessert. "Thanks for the tip." It was time to kiss up a little after her run-in with the celebrity chef at the opening ceremonies. "I appreciate learning from such an accomplished chef."

Hugh leaned toward Dani. He seemed to forget that he had yelled at her earlier for eavesdropping because he lowered his voice and said, "There's so much I could teach you." He waggled his brows. "Maybe a private lesson tonight?"

"That would be inappropriate before the contest." Amelia nudged her employer. "Unless you included all the contestants."

Hugh's face reddened and he snapped, "Of course! That's what I meant."

* * *

They were running late. After they finished eating, people had descended on their table, all wanting an autograph and their picture taken with Hugh.

At first, he'd tried to refuse, but Amelia whispered in his ear, and he'd pasted a smile on his face and started signing napkins.

Finally, about four o'clock, a full hour after they were scheduled to have been done with lunch, Wallace's staff stepped in and started moving the group out of the restaurant and into their cars. Everyone was instructed to meet back at the union where Wallace would give them a brief tour of the facilities and then they'd have a chance to do a trial run of their recipes.

Dani was in the last group of people to be ushered outside. She followed the contest staffer leading them to the parking lot, then headed to her van.

She had just found her car key and unlocked the van when she heard squealing tires and then an ominous thud.

Chapter 8

Dani froze. That had sounded like a bad accident.

Loud cursing jumpstarted her heart and she ran from between the cars. Skidding to a stop, she scanned the parking lot trying to figure out where the crash had occurred. Another torrent of profanity drew her to the next row over, where a man lay on the asphalt clutching his leg and moaning.

When Dani got closer, she saw that it was Elvis.

He spotted her and yelled, "Did you see that car? It came out of nowhere and mowed me down."

"Sorry, no." Dani rushed over to him. "Let me call for an ambulance."

Elvis held up his hand. "Nah, I don't think anything's broken. Just help me up."

"That's not a good idea." Dani shook her head and took her cell phone from her pocket.

Elvis grabbed her arm and used it to get to his feet. "See. I'm standing. If I go to the hospital, they might not let me compete."

"Well…" Dani hesitated. She wasn't his mom, and he was a grown man, she couldn't force him to accept treatment. "But we do need to get the police here to report the hit-and-run."

Elvis looked her in the eye. "If we do that, neither of us will have time to practice our recipes."

The guy had a point. Dani's conscience nagged at her to call 911 anyway, but her common sense told her she really needed to make her chili at least one more time before the contest tomorrow.

Evidently sensing her weakening, Elvis wheedled, "How about you give me a ride and then afterwards we can stop at the police station and file a report?"

Dani scanned the asphalt. There were no tire marks, and she didn't see any debris so there wasn't any evidence for the police to gather.

Maybe Spencer would know the right thing to do. She tried his number, but her call went right to voice mail. Next, she dialed Gray Christensen. He might not be in town, but he could still advise her on her best course of action. Unfortunately, he didn't answer either.

"Shoot." Dani stared at Elvis. "Are you sure you're alright?"

"They only clipped me. I'll have a heck of bruise on my shin, but I can walk." He hobbled a few steps back and forth. "See."

Dani knew she shouldn't, but she said, "Okay, then we'd better get going or we'll miss the tour and the chance to do a dry run."

Elvis started to limp toward Dani but stopped and stuffed the slip of paper that he'd been holding into the front pocket of his jeans.

Dani waited for an explanation, but he avoided her stare and continued toward the van. Once he was inside, she dug out her first aid kit and gave him an instant ice pack. Then she slid behind the wheel, started the motor, backed up, and headed toward the university.

As she drove, Dani sighed. This was a heck of a kickoff for the challenge. She could only hope that a rocky start meant a smooth finish.

* * *

As soon as they arrived at the union, Dani looked around for Spencer. She spotted him in a heated conversation with a young man she presumed was a student. The wind was whipping the guy's long black hair around his head like a tornado, and he seemed frustrated with both it and Spencer.

Dani stepped within hearing range as Spencer said, "Don't think of it as a competition, Quest. Not only will pots of the contestants' practice chili go to the food pantry to feed people in need, but samples of the finished product will be offered free to the spectators." Spencer smiled. "My girlfriend tells me that food is an expression of love."

Quest clenched his fist. "True love would be all the contestants sharing the prize."

"Sorry." Spencer backed away. "There's nothing I can do about that."

Quest fumed. "The winner should be made to donate the money to charity."

"Again," Spencer turned away, "not something the university can control."

Quest pulled out his cell phone and stomped off, glaring at Dani as he passed her.

She looked up and saw that Spencer had caught her eavesdropping. She made a face and joked, "Sounds like you're not having a very good day."

"An understatement if I ever heard one." Spencer walked over and kissed her on the cheek. "Between him and the other yahoo protesting the use of meat and animal products, I missed the luncheon. And I had wheedled a seat at your table too. Was it good?"

Dani tilted her hand back and forth. "The food was fine, but the company was only so-so."

"Oh?" Spencer's eyebrows drew together. "Why is that?"

She rolled her eyes. "Hugh Granville managed to be both condescending and a *letch*."

"What did he do?" Spencer's head swiveled as he scanned the crowd.

"Just a stupid come-on line. Nothing to worry about." Dani frowned. "But he was darn insulting to Elvis."

"The big guy?"

Dani nodded, then hit her forehead with her palm. "Which reminds me. He and I were among the last to leave the restaurant, and when Elvis went to get his car, someone ran him over then fled the scene."

"Is he okay?"

"He says he is, and he wouldn't let me call for an ambulance or the police, because he was afraid that we'd be late for the next challenge activity."

Spencer grimaced. "You mean you two just left?"

"Yeah." Dani knew she was in the wrong, but hoped Spencer wouldn't make too big a deal about it. "I felt since Elvis was the victim and I hadn't seen anything, it was up to him. He rode with me here and after we're finished, we'll stop at the police station and report it."

Before Spencer could respond, there was an announcement for all contestants and judges to meet in the union lobby for a tour of the facilities.

"Gotta go!" Dani gave Spencer a quick kiss and dashed away.

The tour was led by Wallace Zorillo and, as they walked, he said, "All the equipment has been provided by my company."

During their lunch, the patio had been transformed. Eight cooking stations now ringed the area. Each competitor had a long table, an electrical outlet strip, a small refrigerator, a shelving unit filled with the supplies and equipment they'd brought with them, and a four-burner cooktop.

Wallace gestured to the arrangements. "Please find your assigned spot and check to see if there's anything else you need."

While the contestants were looking over their stations, Wallace explained that they'd had to run two miles of cable to provide the electricity needed for the setup and had rented ranges powered by portable propane tanks. He also mentioned that if the weather turned bad, they had a second setup ready in the union's largest ballroom.

The judges and the media were seated in the center of the patio. The judges were shielded from sight by several folding screens, but the media had an unobstructed view of the contestants. Spectators would be allowed to stroll through the area.

Dani was impressed by the professional arrangements and amazed at how nicely the contest space had been designed. Her previous apartment had a less well-appointed kitchen.

Contestants were arranged alphabetically by

state. This put Dani between Tory from California and Jill from Kansas. She cringed. They'd been the two women arguing in the restroom and both glared at her as she took her place.

Wallace waited a few minutes, then asked, "Everyone happy?" When they all murmured yes, he said, "Okay, you'll have three hours for your trial run. This will enable you to make sure you have everything you need for tomorrow. No one today, including the judges, will taste your chili. Please place the finished product in the slow cookers provided and it will be served by the food pantry tonight. Do not put your name or any identifying marks on the container."

Dani smiled. When Spencer had told her he'd arranged for the donation to the food pantry in order to appease the Social and Economic Realities Foundation as well as the Peace and Love Network, she'd been pleased to hear the chili would go to a good cause and not be wasted.

Turning to her cook station, Dani reached for a pan to begin browning her ground turkey. But as she pulled it from the shelf she yelped and jumped back.

Standing behind Dani's shelving unit was a girl dressed in faded jeans and an old army jacket zipped all the way up. Her white-blonde hair was tucked under a baseball cap. Removing her sunglasses, she shot Dani a wide grin.

Dani stood frozen. What in the world was Atti doing at the Chili Challenge? And more importantly, had she brought Khan with her? A dog might get Dani disqualified.

Chapter 9

Atti leaned forward and said, "I thought you'd never get here. Some guy was nosing around your station."

"What do you mean by nosing around?" Dani asked.

Atti twitched her shoulders. "I got here a little before everyone started trickling in after lunch and this dude the size of a grizzly bear was poking through your stuff. He even opened your refrigerator."

"Did he take anything?"

Puffing out her chest, Atti shook her head. "I asked what the eff he thought he was doing, and he ran away with his tail between his legs."

"What did he do then?" Dani asked, worried she'd been singled out for sabotage.

Atti moved closer. "He waited until another dude raised a fuss with Spencer, then he went through everyone's stuff and took notes."

Dani hesitated, then stepped out from behind her table and scanned the patio. Spencer had disappeared, but she spotted Wallace Zorillo, and with Atti trailing her like a piece of toilet paper stuck to her shoe, she headed toward him.

Pausing before she reached the head honcho, Dani asked, "You didn't bring Khan, did you?"

"No. Ivy and Laz took him to the dog park." Atti tugged on her arm until they were facing each other. "I figured you'd need me here to watch over you. You and the other girls are too nice. None of you look out for number one."

"Oh, I don't think that's necessary for a little cooking contest," Dani managed to say in a neutral tone. All she needed was a paranoid Atti around. Crossing her fingers for the lie she was about to tell, Dani said, "The other contestants all seem really nice."

"In that case, there's no problem." Atti hoisted her jeans up a fraction. "If everyone behaves, I'll just get to sample lots of good chili. If they don't, I'll be here to make things right."

Ever since Dani rescued Atti from the homeless camp and gave her a place to live, Atti had been extremely grateful. Then when Dani had arranged a scholarship for the teen at the local community college, Atti had become Dani's fiercest protector.

"That's very sweet of you." Dani gave Atti her best fake smile, all the while praying the girl wouldn't cause any trouble.

Excuses raced through Dani's mind, but she

couldn't come up with any way to get Atti to leave, so she'd just have to keep an eye on her. But right now, she needed to inform Mr. Zorillo about the guy Atti had spotted.

* * *

The company president had been concerned with Dani's story and made an announcement asking everyone to check their equipment and ingredients. None of the contestants had found anything amiss, and Dani had returned to her station to start cooking.

She propped her tablet up on its stand, then began gathering what she needed. She ticked off the components as she placed them on the table.

"Ground turkey?" Atti gazed at the package of meat Dani had just taken from the mini fridge. "Why are you using that?"

"I tried both beef and pork, but it seems that the turkey takes the smoky flavor better."

Dani glanced at her recipe and turned to the shelves containing her dry ingredients. The container of peanut butter was on the top all the way in the back, and she couldn't quite reach it.

She looked around for something to stand on and spotted a folding chair off to the side. Setting it up next to the shelves, she gingerly climbed onto the seat.

Dani had just curled her fingers around the jar

when she heard someone scream, "Son of a B—!"

Startled, Dani threw her arms in the air trying to regain her balance. She failed and an instant later, she ended up sprawled on the cement as tiny bottles of spices rained down on her head like brightly colored hailstones.

As Atti helped her up, Dani looked around just in time to see Jill VanAsden, the soccer mom, rush out of her station waving a dripping Styrofoam tray. "Someone switched my ground sirloin with a block of mushy crap!"

Jill paused and looked around. When no one admitted to the crime, she cursed at the top of her lungs and threatened to kick a goal using the culprit's head as a ball as soon as she found out who did it.

While Dani and Atti stood watching the drama, Jill ran past and thumped the oozing package on Tory Mays table like a gavel. "I know you did this, Ms. Yoga Queen, and you're not getting away with it."

As Dani plucked a miniature bottle of her homemade ancho chili pepper from her cleavage, she toyed with the idea of pretending she hadn't noticed the commotion and getting on with her cooking. Which would have been a good plan if, just as Dani was turning away, Wallace and Spencer hadn't come charging over.

Considering her station was sandwiched

between Tory's and Jill's, Dani gave up any idea of remaining uninvolved. Wading through the spice bottles, she moved to her table and looked to her left.

Atti joined her, shooting out questions faster than a machine gun. "What's with those two? Why would she switch her meat? What're they going to do about it?"

Dani wished she knew. She was afraid it might involve canceling the contest.

A crowd was gathering, including the journalists covering the event. Jill stood in the center of the group waving a fistful of dripping meat-like substance in the air. Spencer was attempting to disarm her, and Wallace's face was so red Dani was afraid he was about to have a stroke.

Ruben Caballero had his arm around Tory who was sobbing but taking a break every so often to taunt Jill. "You probably did it yourself trying to get me kicked out of the contest."

Jill's eyes narrowed when Wallace stepped up to her and said, "Earlier, I asked all contestants to check their ingredients, why didn't you notice the substitution at that time?"

"I saw the package of ground beef," Jill stammered, "and it seemed like it was fine and I—I don't feel so good." She waved a hand in front of her face. "I think, I'm going to faint."

Wallace took her arm and eased her into a chair that had miraculously appeared. "Just calm down. We'll get you a new package of meat." He turned to face the people who were watching the drama unfold and said, "In fact, any contestant that would like something replaced should make a list. My employees will go to the nearest supermarket and buy whatever you need. Once they return, the time will then start for your trial run." He snapped his fingers and a pudgy blond man appeared at his elbow. "Bert, here, will be in charge of making sure that you're completely satisfied."

"But I want her punished." Jill pointed at Tory, who stared back.

Before Wallace could respond, a sweet female voice managed to project itself over the noise. "Oh, my heavens. What in the world is going on around here?"

The crowd parted and Latoya Lin walked through. Jill and Tory tried to explain at once, but Latoya raised her plump hand for silence.

"You all are giving me palpitations, and I'd hate to have to go to the hospital and miss judging your chili."

Both women's mouths shut so fast, their teeth clanked.

Dani stared at Latoya and thought she saw an

impish twinkle in the woman's eyes.

Jill and Tory tried to speak again, and this time Latoya's snapped, "Ladies, you are about to screw up this contest and be asked to leave. Is that what you want?"

Dani barely stopped herself from snorting. Latoya didn't mince words and now both women wore identical appalled expressions.

"Please forgive me." Jill put the package of meat on the table and stepped back. "I was just upset, but I'd like to take Mr. Zorillo's kind offer to replace my ground sirloin and start over."

Latoya clasped Jill's hands. "Thank you, my dear. That's so sweet of you."

"But..." Jill tightened her grip on the older woman's fingers, "...we do have to discover who substituted this fake meat for my prime beef."

Tory shook off Ruben and took Latoya's other hand. "Yes, we do. I want my name cleared."

"Of course." Latoya maintained her smile as she freed herself from their grasps. "I'm sure our wonderful head of campus security will discover the culprit before the challenge is over." She turned to the crowd. "One of the reasons contestants like this have trial runs the day before the actual cook-off is to iron out any kinks, to find the mistakes, and make everything perfect for the actual competition."

The crowd broke into applause.

Dani was reaching for her cast iron frying pan when she heard a male voice roar, "Dammit to hell! Who switched my jalapeños for serranos?"

Dani froze until another voice shouted, "Who screwed with my timer?"

Within the next few minutes several other contestants added their complaints to the general din.

Dani's heart sank. Who was sabotaging the contestants' recipes and why?

Chapter 10

It had taken hours for the chaos to die down. Those who had their stuff messed with had to be soothed, and new ingredients had to be obtained for everyone.

While all that was happening, Spencer called in several of his off-duty security officers. None of his people were thrilled with the forced overtime, but the newest hire, Warren Douglas, was livid.

"Man, one of the reasons I quit my last job was that I was always being yanked in to cover a shift." Douglas huffed, his cheeks jiggling in outrage.

Spencer narrowed his eyes. "Did you read the contract you signed?"

"Yeah." Douglas's pale complexion reddened, and he stared at his shoes. "Sort of."

Crossing his arms, Spencer barely held on to his temper. "We don't often have situations that require additional personnel, but when we do, all officers are expected to make themselves available."

"What if I was sick or out of town?" Douglas ran his fingers through his short brown hair, then tugged at his goatee.

Spencer clenched his teeth. "Then you would be

excused." He looked at the rest of his officers who were nervously shuffling their feet. "Anyone else have a question or a problem?"

When they each shook their head, he assigned them to patrol the patio's perimeter, then said, "If someone attempts to enter the contestants' cooking areas you are to detain them and radio me."

"What if they resist?" Douglas's eyes gleamed. "Can we cuff them?"

Spencer paused. They had the authority, but something about Douglas's eagerness made him hesitate.

Finally, he said, "No rough stuff. If they run off, let them go. Only use the cuffs if they try to get past you and into the contest space."

* * *

More than half of the competitors were still trying to finish their dishes at six o'clock when Wallace Zorillo grabbed the mike.

There was a brief electronic screech, then the company president announced, "Supper will be pushed back to eight so that you can complete your trial run and still enjoy the dinner being provided for you in the small ballroom." He cleared his throat. "Because of the difficulties we ran into this afternoon, you will all be allowed to come here tomorrow morning to practice your recipe again. Your areas will be available to you from 6 a.m. until 9 a.m. At that point, the stations will be cleaned and restocked, and, as previously planned, the contest will start at ten."

As Zorillo spoke, Spencer strolled through the patio hoping to hear something that would give him a clue as to who was behind the sabotage, but there were only a few sighs of relief and a couple of grumbles. Nothing that pointed him in the direction of the culprit.

He was nearing the French doors that led into the union when a young man and woman rushed out onto the patio. The guy was well over six feet tall, skinny, and wore horn-rimmed glasses. The girl was nearly his complete opposite — six inches shorter, well-rounded, with long wavy brown hair.

Spencer clenched his teeth. Just what he needed. Justin Boward and Frannie Ryan worked for the local paper, and they had a habit of turning up at the worst times. Why were they just arriving rather than leaving like the other reporters covering the event?

The duo skidded to a stop in front of Spencer, and Frannie asked breathlessly, "Where's Dani?"

Several questions crowded Spencer's lips, but he finally managed to push one out in front of the others. "Why are you looking for her?"

"Because of the fire," Justin answered. "Someone lit up the dumpster behind the carriage house."

Spencer grimaced. "How bad is it?"

"We got it out with one of the fire extinguishers Dani keeps all over. And since the dumpster is away from the building and across a concrete pad there was no damage."

"Any idea who the firebug is?"

Both Frannie and Justin shrugged.

"It was probably a random act of vandalism," Spencer said, hoping that was the case.

Justin and Frannie looked at each other. Finally, she gave an almost imperceptible nod, and Justin said, "*The Normalton News* has been getting letters to the editor urging people to take action against the Route 66 Rally. This morning, there was another one from someone who said they were going to teach the Chili Challenge contestants a lesson for being a part of the event."

Before Spencer could respond, Atti popped up from wherever she'd been lurking and said, "Whoever's behind it must be escalating their tactics. First, the stuff here, and now a fire. Dani needs to drop out of the contest."

"Are you going to tell her that?" Spencer retorted. "Because I'm not going to do it and be accused of being sexist."

Atti studied the ground and mumbled, "We've got to protect her."

"And we will." Spencer planned on sticking to Dani like a wet shower curtain until this whole shebang was over. And if he wasn't available, he'd make darn sure she was never alone. He looked at the reporters. "Did you call the police or the fire department?"

Both Frannie and Justin developed an intense interest in their shoes, and she muttered, "We didn't see the point. The fire was out and it's not as if anyone is going to be too concerned about burned trash."

"Well then…" Spencer hated to admit it, but the reporters were right. With no destruction of property or injuries, the cops and the firefighters had better things to do than investigate something that could be attributed to kids messing around. "I guess it's up to my security team to catch whoever's doing this."

Frannie nodded. "Dani's the only local contestant, so the rest are all staying in the union's guest rooms. At least they're all together."

"Right," Spencer acknowledged. "And it means they'll be hard for anyone to get at since you need a key card to operate the elevators to the guest room floors."

Spencer saw Justin swallow hard. He knew the young man was not comfortable around him and gave him a slight chin jerk to go ahead.

"Well, the thing is, the person doing this could just wait until a contestant uses their key card, get into the elevator, and ride along."

The muscle under Spencer's right eye twitched. The kid was right. "I'll instruct all contestants to make sure they don't allow anyone who is unknown to them to board their elevator."

"The judges and some of the media are staying in those guest rooms too." Justin dug in the pocket of his jeans, pulled out a crumpled piece of paper, and thrust it at Spencer. "I printed out the list."

"Thanks." Spencer didn't bother asking how Justin had gotten his hands on it. The kid was a computer genius and hacking into the union's files would be a piece of cake. "You wouldn't happen to have a copy of that letter, would you?"

Justin grabbed his cell phone from his back pocket, swiped a couple of times, then when his thumbs quit flying, he handed the device to Spencer.

SINCE THE UNIVERSITY CONTINUES TO PANDER TO THE ROUTE 66 ORGANIZATION, WE HAVE BEEN FORCED TO TAKE ACTION. OUR ADMINISTRATION SHOULD NEVER HAVE ALLOWED THE CHILI CHALLENGE ON CAMPUS AS IT GOES AGAINST THE SCHOOL'S CORE VALUES. WE MUST MAKE AN EXAMPLE OF THIS SACRILEGE. PARTICIPANTS BEWARE!

Spencer stared at the brief message. What kind of lunatic wrote something like that about a chili cook-off?

Atti had been reading over Spencer's shoulder. "That's just crazy sauce."

"Which makes it even more alarming." Spencer looked around for Wallace Zorillo and spotted the head honcho by the podium. "Time to rally the troops."

Chapter 11

Dani had just put her finished chili into one of the eight slow cookers that would be taken to the food pantry, when she heard the PA system crackle. She looked toward the podium and saw Spencer holding the microphone.

"May I have your attention, please?" His usual smooth baritone had an edge to it and his jet-black hair was sticking up as if he'd been running his fingers through the short strands.

Dani grimaced. Something was definitely wrong.

All conversations stopped and Spencer announced, "I have been notified that a warning against the Chili Challenge event has been emailed to the local newspaper."

There was a gasp from the crowd and a frisson of fear ran up Dani's spine.

"As you all know, most threats of this sort are nothing but hot air, but because we have had some vandalism involving your equipment and ingredients, I have increased our security measures. In order to keep everyone safe, I advise you all to employ the buddy system. Also, do not ride the elevators with any strangers, keep your rooms locked at all times, and check the peephole before opening your doors."

Hands waved and Spencer nodded to Mick Owen. The judges had been sitting together and the cookbook author stood. "Chief Drake, I take it the threats include anyone involved with the contest, not just the contestants."

"That's correct. The letter said 'participants,' so that could mean anyone with an official connection to the event." Spencer gazed around the patio, briefly meeting Dani's stare. "With the exception of Chef Sloan, all the competitors, judges, and Mr. Zorillo's employees are staying in the union guest rooms, which means I advise you all to take the precautions I've outlined.

Hugh Granville shot to his feet. "I demand a personal bodyguard. As a celebrity, I am the obvious target."

Spencer's lips thinned, but he nodded. "I'll assign one of my security officers to you."

"Any idea what this saboteur has against the Chili Challenge?" Latoya Lin asked.

Spencer hesitated, then said, "There were a few student groups that for various reasons objected to the event." He smiled reassuringly. "However, I met with their representatives and certain concessions were made to alleviate their concerns. Still, I will be looking into those organizations."

"Can't you trace the email?" the engineer from Texas asked.

"I don't have access to the newspaper's computers, and while I will request it, I'm guessing either it will be refused or tied up in red tape too long to be useful."

After answering a few more questions, Spencer handed the mike over to Wallace.

"While I understand if anyone wishes to withdraw from the contest, and my assistant will be happy to help you with travel arrangements, I hope you will remain." When no one came forward, the company president added, "I have notified the police, and they, along with campus security, will be investigating."

With that, people began drifting away. Dani noticed that while most of the judges and contestants were keeping together as they headed inside to go to their rooms, the lawyer from Oklahoma left by himself.

Dani returned to her station. She had already switched everything off, cleaned up, and made a list of what she wanted to bring with her the next day, but she needed to grab her purse from where she had tucked it under the bottom shelf.

When she straightened, Spencer and Atti were

waiting for her. Dani didn't like the anger in Atti's brown eyes or the worry in Spencer's blue ones as she waited for one of them to speak.

Atti held out her hand. "Give me the keys to your van and I'll drive it back to the house for you."

"Why?"

"I thought I'd take you and Elvis to the police station," Spencer said. "Now that we know about that email, his hit-and-run takes on a more ominous meaning." He looked around. "Where is he?"

Dani shrugged. "He must have gone to his room."

Spencer took out his cell phone and dialed. "This is Campus Security Chief Drake, please connect me with Elvis Larson."

Dani could hear the phone ringing and ringing, and she watched Spencer's expression darken.

He disconnected. "He's not answering."

"Maybe someone gave him a lift to pick up his car at the restaurant," Dani offered. "He's probably going to the PD on his own since I didn't see anything."

Spencer nodded, then dialed again. "Spencer Drake for Chief Cleary." A few seconds later, he said, "Chief, I'm not sure if you're aware that we have a situation with the Chili Challenge at the university."

Dani chewed her thumbnail as Spencer

explained, then asked about Elvis. His frown grew deeper as he listened.

"Thanks, Chief. I will." He put his phone away and looked at Dani. "No report of any hit-and-run has been made today. I'd better check Elvis's room."

"Don't you need a warrant?"

"School officials can enter the room to perform a visual inspection," Spencer explained. "And the agreement that all guests sign when renting a room in the union also gives us the right to search closets and drawers."

Dani raised an eyebrow. "I bet there are very few people who read that form before signing."

"Their loss." Spencer smirked. "Why don't you come with me to check on Elvis, then I can give you a ride home afterwards."

"Sure." Dani handed over the keys to her van to Atti, then warned, "Drive carefully and go straight home."

"Yes, ma'am." Atti saluted, turned, and jogged away.

Spencer opened the door that led from the patio into the union and Dani walked through. They stopped by the guest rooms check-in desk where Spencer got Elvis's room number and picked up a passkey, then they rode the elevator to the top floor.

Elvis's room was only a few feet down the hall

from the elevator. Dani stood behind Spencer as he knocked on the door and announced his identity.

When there was no response, he gestured for her to try, so she raised her voice and said, "Elvis, it's me, Dani Sloan. We're just checking to make sure you're okay."

After a minute or two of silence, Spencer used the key card and cautiously opened the door. It was a typical hotel room with a king size bed taking up most of the space. There was no sign that anyone occupied the room.

Spencer checked the closet, dresser, and the bathroom, but they were all empty. If Elvis had ever been there, he'd taken his belongings and gone.

"Did he say if he was staying in the room the challenge provided?" Spencer asked.

"It didn't come up in the conversation." Dani stared into the bathroom. "But, unless housekeeping really stinks, I think he was here." She pointed at the toilet paper. "It doesn't have the corner folded." Then she gestured to the sink. "And the soap is unwrapped and used."

Spencer nodded. "Good observation."

"Thanks." Dani backed out of the room. "What should we do?"

Spencer pursed his lips. "Let's check to see if his car is still at the restaurant."

"How will you know which one is Elvis's?" Dani asked as they headed to Spencer's truck.

"Remember the temporary parking permit you received? They were issued through Campus Security, so I have a list of all the participants' vehicles."

Dani was silent as they headed toward the café. Beyond exhausted, she mindlessly watched the buildings fly by as they drove.

After finding the Apple of Eden's lot completely empty and realizing there wasn't anything else they could do to locate the missing grill master, Dani said, "I need to get home. We're supposed to be at the dinner by eight and it's already past seven. Drop me off and come back in forty-five minutes."

It was only a few minutes to the house Dani had inherited from Geraldine Cook. Geraldine had been Dani's late grandmother's sorority sister and lifelong friend. The two women had taken some kind of oath to look out for each other's families, so when Gerry had died childless, she left the place to Dani.

A few weeks before she'd found out about Mrs. Cook's bequest, Dani had quit her job in the HR department of Homeland Insurance. Thus, when she'd gotten the unexpected windfall, she decided that instead of looking for a new position, she'd take advantage of her stroke of luck and start a business doing what she really loved: cooking.

The instant Spencer's truck stopped, Dani said a hasty goodbye, jumped out, and headed up the steps. She paused on the porch to dig through her purse for the keys, then quickly unlocked the door and went inside.

Taking the stairs two at a time, she rushed into her suite and kicked off her shoes. Dani hurriedly stripped, showered, and, after she was dry, she put on her underwear and bra. She then grabbed the dress she had already selected from its hanger.

As she pulled it over head and started to shimmy into it, she heard her cell phone chime. The dress was a straight black sheath and required some time to get on. Rushing was not an option, and before she was able to poke her head out of the draped neckline, she heard two more chimes.

Dani hurried to her discarded pants and dug the phone from the pocket. Grabbing the receiver, she heard a male voice say, "Dani—" Then an extremely loud buzzing sound crackled through the speaker, and she couldn't decipher another word.

She shouted into the device, "Hang up and call back."

After disconnecting, she waited, but when nothing happened, she checked the number that had called. It wasn't one she recognized.

Grinding her teeth, Dani finally gave up and went back to dressing. It only took her a few minutes to finish. She slipped on her black pumps, applied concealer under her eyes and mascara on her lashes, then put her hair into a topknot.

She inserted silver hoops in her ears and stuffed her wallet and phone into her evening bag.

As she descended the stairs, Dani looked at her watch. It was ten to eight and she hadn't heard a doorbell. Unless one of her boarders had let Spencer in before he had even rung the bell, he was late, which wasn't at all like him.

As she stood waiting for Spencer to arrive, she checked her cell. She'd received a text from an unfamiliar number.

SORRY TO BAIL ON THE CONTEST. THANKS FOR HELPING WHEN THAT CAR HIT ME. HOPE WE MEET AGAIN.

Evidently, Elvis had left the building.

Chapter 12

Shortly after receiving Elvis's text, Dani's cell chirped indicating she had a message in her voice mail. Considering her phone had been in her hand the whole time, she wasn't sure how she'd missed a call.

Punching in her code, she recognized Spencer's voice. "What's wrong with your phone? My calls keep going directly to voice mail. Anyway, I've had an emergency come up and I can't take you to the dinner." There was a pause, and she could hear a muffled voice in the background, then Spencer said, "I spoke to Ivy and Laz, they'll drive you to the union, but it will take them a bit to get to the house. Please don't go by yourself. I'll be there to take you home." There was silence, but she could tell he hadn't hung up, then he added, "I hope."

"Damn!" Dani hated being late.

Her head felt like it was about to explode. She was tired and cranky and just wanted to stay at home and have ice cream for supper.

Did Spencer's emergency involve Elvis's disappearance? She quickly forwarded Spencer the message she received from him, then stomped into the parlor to wait for her bodyguards.

Checking her watch every few seconds, Dani gritted her teeth. "Where are they?" Beyond annoyed, her voice rose as she talked to herself. "Five more minutes and I'm leaving with or without them!"

Starr Fleming, one of Dani's boarders, stepped into the parlor. The clicking of the beads woven into her braids announced her presence even before she asked, "Are you okay?"

"I'm fine." She took a deep breath and forced herself to smile calmly. "Just a little frustrated."

Starr edged closer. "Why are you sitting in here?"

Usually, Dani only used the parlor to entertain clients. The antique furniture was far from comfortable and the atmosphere too formal for anyone to really relax.

"Waiting for my ride. I figured that I could run out when I heard their car." Dani leaned her head back on the settee, feeling strangely like crying. "The rest is a long story." She described the day's events, then rubbed her temples. "I'm not sure why I'm making such a big deal about waiting for Ivy and Laz to show up. It's not as if the teacher will mark me tardy."

Starr chuckled, then her brown eyes softened. "I'm happy to drive you," she offered. "Robert had to cancel our date." She smiled. "At least now I know what's going on. For a second there, I was afraid Robert was ghosting me. Spencer needing to call in all his security guys at the last minute explains everything."

Robert Porter, Starr's boyfriend, worked for campus security. After a stint in the military, he'd taken the job to supplement his income while taking classes at the university to finish his BA degree.

"Robert would never dump you that way. He's too much of a stand-up guy." Dani inhaled and instantly felt a bit calmer. "And thanks for the offer of a ride, but I'm sure Ivy and Laz will be here soon."

"Who do you think is sabotaging the Chili Challenge?" Starr perched on the edge of one of the Eastlake chairs.

Dani wrinkled her brow. "Spencer thought it might be a member of one of those activist groups that lodged a complaint with the university about the rally. But now that one of the contestants has pulled a Houdini, I wonder if it has something to do with him."

"Or maybe he was afraid and decided a chance at winning the contest wasn't worth the risk." Starr, played with one of her braids.

Dani bit her lip. "I suppose. But Elvis didn't strike me as someone who would be scared very easily."

Before Starr could respond, Ivy slammed open the front door and yelled, "Dani!"

"I'm right here." Dani jumped from the settee, said goodbye to Starr, and hurried into the foyer. "Let's go."

* * *

"Love, I promise, I'll totally tell her as soon as this contest is over. She'd nick everything in the joint accounts if I told her now." A posh male voice Dani recognized as belonging to Hugh Granville drifted out of a short hallway leading to the bathrooms.

Dani was trapped. She didn't want to eavesdrop, but she was waiting for the elevator in the union and there wasn't anywhere else to stand.

She hesitated. Maybe she should take the stairs.

No. When Laz and Ivy had dropped her at the union, she'd promised she'd take the elevator straight to the ballroom.

Before she could figure out which was worse, eavesdropping or breaking her word to Ivy and Laz, the chef's assistant, Amelia, snapped, "You always have some excuse. Why didn't you finalize the change before we left California?"

"I don't see why you're in such a rush." Hugh's voice took on a cajoling tone. "I'll keep my bloody promise. You'll be my hostess on next season's show. I just need to convince Eliza that it's her idea, so she doesn't divorce me and get half my assets."

"You'll do that as soon as we get back?"

The elevator chimed, and Dani cringed when Hugh gasped, "Did you hear that?"

"Hear what?" Amelia asked.

There was a long moment of silence while Dani willed the elevator doors to open so that she could escape without being seen.

"Guess it was nothing," Hugh answered. "But with that wanker causing all the trouble, we'd better get back upstairs to the ballroom. Don't want to get into a dodgy situation on our own."

"Right. Safety in numbers."

Dani sighed with relief as the elevator door slid open and she hurried inside. She stabbed the Close button, but nothing happened, and an instant later, Hugh and Amelia stepped inside the car.

They all nodded at one another, then faced forward and stared at the numbers. It was the longest ride ever, and it was only up to the third floor.

As soon as the door opened, Amelia and Hugh rushed out of the elevator. Dani dawdled, walking as slowly as possible down the hall to allow the celebrity chef and his assistant to enter the ballroom a good minute or two before she followed them.

Making her way into the large area that had been set with circular tables, she shook her head. It didn't sound as if Amelia and her boss were in a romantic relationship, but he was still firing his wife and replacing her with his assistant. Did his assistant have something on the chef?

Shrugging, Dani pushed the scene out of her mind and looked around. The tables were packed, and the servers were scurrying around delivering bowls of steaming soup, bringing baskets of fragrant bread, and filling glasses with wine. Dani's stomach growled. She hadn't had anything to eat since lunch nearly eight hours ago.

She scanned the chairs looking for her assigned seat until one of the servers asked, "Can I help you find your table, ma'am?"

"That would be great."

"Are you a contestant, media, judge, or USE staff?"

"Contestant."

"The contestants are seated two to a table, with their guests, one judge, one media, and two staff." The young man pointed to a group of tables near the rear wall. "Starting from the right side, the places are arranged alphabetically by state."

"Thank you." Dani nodded at the server and walked toward the area he indicated.

She found her place at the second table. Jade Lawrence, the contestant from New Mexico sat next to a handsome man in his fifties. Dani frowned. Alphabetically, she should be seated with the Kansas contestant. The lifestyle coach should have been with Missouri's competitor, which had been Elvis.

The cookbook author, Mick Owen, was chatting with the couple and the remainder of the occupied seats were taken by three people Dani didn't recognize, but assumed were media and staff.

Dani paused only a second before sliding into one of the two empty chairs.

"Are you by yourself?" Jade asked. The woman's skin was stretched across her cheekbones like a drumhead and her eyes bulged like two poached eggs.

"Yes and no." Dani chose her words carefully, not wanting to alarm her tablemates. "My date was called away on business, but I texted my father to join me. He should be here soon."

"I heard that yummy Chief Drake was your boyfriend." Jade arched a brow, then frowned. "Did something else happen with the contest?"

"He didn't say." Dani hurriedly added, "But since he's responsible for the entire campus, it could really be anything."

"I see." Jade patted the man at her side and said, "This is my husband, Eli." She gestured around the table. "You know our distinguished judge Mick."

Dani nodded and Mick took over. "Next to me is Scottie Diller from the local radio station, her soundman, Roger, and Mavis Simpson, our Route 66 Rally liaison."

"Hi, everyone." Dani waved. "I'm Dani Sloan owner of Chef-to-Go and the contestant from Illinois. Sorry I was a little late."

"With all the stuff going on, we were worried something had happened," Jade commented.

"I was waiting for my ride." Dani shrugged. "Chief Drake didn't want me driving here on my own."

Jade wrinkled her brow. "Why?"

"He was just being cautious." Dani smiled. "Like he told all of you, it's safer not to be alone until they've assessed the threat."

The others had remained silent through the exchange, but as Jade paused in her interrogation and Dani sipped from her glass of water, Scottie piped up. "Would you be willing to do a sound bite for my station tomorrow morning before you start your practice round, Dani?"

Dani considered the offer. If she could mention her business, it would be free advertising. She'd just have to make sure she steered away from anything to do with the sabotage and Elvis's disappearance.

"Sure." Dani beamed at Scottie. "I'd love to."

Jade dabbed her lips with her napkin. "I'd be happy to talk to your listeners as well. I am, after all, a doctor of nutrition and a certified life coach."

Eli had been silent, but he cleared his throat and said, "Honey, I don't think that's a good idea. You don't want to draw a target on yourself."

Jade opened her mouth, but then closed it. From her expression, she seemed torn.

Before anyone else could speak, their salads arrived.

As they passed around the bowls of dressing, Mavis leaned toward Dani and said in a low voice, "Be careful of Scottie. She's a bit of a shock jock."

"I had no idea."

"Yes." Mavis tittered. "And even essential oils can't fix her kind of crazy."

"Really?" Dani matched the liaison's low volume. "What has she done?"

"She hasn't been the biggest fan of the Rally. Her radio pieces have mocked the idea of the whole Route 66 allure." Mavis scowled. "It makes you wonder if she has a personal vendetta against the Rally. It would explain the animosity she's shown on her show."

"Thanks for the tip."

"You know," Mavis whispered, "I wouldn't be at all surprised if Scottie was behind the sabotage. You should mention that to your boyfriend."

Dani patted Mavis's hand. "I certainly will."

She smiled reassuringly at the liaison, all the while thinking that she'd tell Spencer about Mavis's theory *after* she'd done the sound bite for the radio station and gotten Chef-to-Go the free advertising.

Chapter 13

Dani's father arrived as the entrées were being served. She hoped he would be happy with Spencer's selection of prime rib. If not, he could have her grilled fish.

Once Jonas was seated and introductions were made, he leaned close to Dani and said quietly, "Have you heard anything from Spencer about the sabotage?"

Dani shook her head.

"If he doesn't get here in time to take you home, I'll drive you." His soothing tenor made Dani relax for the first time since the hit-and-run.

"That would be great. I really do need to make this a relatively early night since I have to get to the Chili Challenge station by five thirty tomorrow."

"We can leave right after dessert."

"Thanks, Dad."

Jonas had canceled his plans to attend the dinner with Dani and was now showing concern for her welfare. He was clearly making an effort to be a better father. Although she didn't completely trust him yet, she was willing to give him a chance to prove himself.

Once they finished their entrées—Jonas had been

more than happy to eat Spencer's prime rib—and the tables were cleared, the room darkened and Wallace Zorillo's voice boomed over the loudspeakers. "Thank you all for hanging in with us. I know the Chili Challenge has been more of a challenge than you expected," he paused for the audiences' polite chuckles, "but both my company and campus security are doing everything possible to ensure your safety. With that in mind, as well as the contestants' early start tomorrow morning, we'll have our apple pie then let everyone go get some rest."

* * *

Dani was used to getting up before sunrise to prepare the Lunch-to-Go meals, but four thirty was early even for her. She stuck an arm out from under the covers and felt around the top of the nightstand for her beeping cell phone.

Turning off the alarm, Dani jumped up. Spencer was picking her up at five fifteen. She was meeting Scottie at five thirty to finish the radio sound bite before six.

Dani wanted the full three hours allotted for practice. And Spencer felt that he had to be at the location anytime the contestants were present.

After setting a new personal record for dressing, Dani hurried downstairs. She turned on the coffee pot, then took a batch of her famous ham muffins out of the freezer and popped them into the microwave. A little while later, when Spencer pulled into the driveway, she was already on the porch with two thermal mugs, a takeaway breakfast, and everything she needed for the contest.

Not waiting for him to get out of the vehicle, she hurried over and placed her box of supplies into the truck bed, then climbed into the passenger side of Spencer's pickup, handed him his cup, and wedged the open container of muffins on the console between them. Settling in, she put her tote bag by her feet and fastened her seatbelt.

"Wow." Spencer leaned over and kissed her cheek. "What a great surprise. I'm starving."

"Help yourself," Dani mumbled around the bite she'd just taken.

"I didn't get a chance for supper last night or anything to eat this morning."

"I figured as much." Dani squirmed in her seat. "We'd better get going."

"I suppose." Spencer expertly backed out of the long drive. "How was the dinner? I was glad your father was there to take you home."

"The food was fine." Dani held a silent debate with herself, then gave in and told Spencer about what Mavis had said about Scottie Diller.

"Sounds like you'll have to be careful during

your interview this morning." Spencer took a gulp of coffee. "Meanwhile, I'll look into Mavis's concern. Anything else I should investigate?"

Dani swallowed another mouthful of muffin and said, "I doubt this has anything to do with what's going on, but Hugh and his assistant were arguing about a change of personnel on his TV program. He promised her that he was firing his wife from her front-of-house role and Amelia would be taking her place."

Spencer was silent for a few seconds before saying, "You're right. It's probably not relevant. That is unless Mrs. Granville is in Normalton."

Dani nodded, then ate the rest of her muffin. "Any of the activist organization leaders seem like a good suspect?"

Spencer shrugged. "None of them have alibis, so…"

"How about Elvis?" Dani asked. "Did you get a hold of him?"

"He's not answering the number on his entry form." Spencer put on his turn signal and slowed down, then drove the truck into the lot behind the union. "I've contacted the local police and asked them to do a wellness check. As soon as we get parked, I'll call and see what they came up with."

When Spencer stopped the pickup, Dani

gathered her things and opened the door. She climbed out and hurried toward the patio. She'd come back for her box after her interview.

Dani had only taken a few steps when she noticed that Spencer was lagging behind her. He was speaking into his cell phone, and she hesitated. Should she wait for him to catch up or continue on her own?

Before she made a decision, a burly guy dressed in a custodian's coverall with a baseball cap pulled low on his forehead rushed past her. He bumped her arm causing her to drop her travel mug but didn't stop to apologize.

Hearing the clatter of the cup against the asphalt, Spencer looked up and yelled for the fleeing man to stop. He ignored him and jogged out of sight.

"No harm done." Dani picked up her mug and waved to Spencer. "Except for a few scratches, it's fine."

Spencer frowned as he caught up with her. "Are you sure?" When she nodded, they continued to walk as he spoke into his phone. "Sorry, what were you saying?"

As Dani and Spencer reached the corner of the building, there was a loud whoosh, then a thundering boom. The ground shook and Dani grabbed Spencer's arm while locking her knees.

She watched in horror as a man ran toward her, screaming. The guy clutched her by the shoulders and, although he was speaking, Dani could only make out a couple of words — explosion and fire.

Spencer pried the man away from Dani, and asked, "What happened?" The guy was shaking so violently he didn't seem aware of his surroundings. "What exploded and where's the fire?"

When the man still didn't respond, Spencer handed his cell to Dani and said, "Call 911."

As soon as the call was answered, Dani reported, "There's been some kind of explosion near the NU union. We need an ambulance and the fire department. I'm not sure exactly what the situation is."

"Units will be there in a few minutes. Please stay on the phone until help arrives." The dispatcher's voice was calm and professional.

"Fine." Dani left the line open.

Spencer was still trying to get answers from the guy who had run up to them, but he wasn't putting together coherent sentences.

Dani noticed that the guy was bleeding from small wounds on his face and hands. They needed a first aid kit.

Still holding Spencer's cell phone, Dani peeked around the building. She could see flames shooting up from the union's patio and guessed the explosion had been one of the propane tanks used to power the portable stoves.

She wasn't sure what to do. Should she try to get inside to find a first aid kit? But the union didn't open for another ninety minutes, so the doors would be locked. And the entrance was right next to the patio. What if there was another explosion?

While she was considering her next move, an earsplitting shriek from the patio prodded her into action, and without thinking, Dani rushed towards the scream. While she ran, she informed the dispatcher of the new developments.

As Dani neared the patio, she saw Scottie Diller. The radio personality stood in the famous *Home Alone* pose, hands to cheeks with mouth and eyes rounded into giant Os.

Looking past the shrieking woman, Dani saw a figure on the ground engulfed in flames.

Chapter 14

Spencer ran around the corner of the building. "What's going on?"

"Someone's on fire!" Dani shouted. "We have to put it out."

He wrenched the tote bag from her shoulder and searched through it, coming up with her chef coat and apron. Without a word, he sprinted past Scottie and threw the coat and apron on the figure on the ground, then shrugged out of his own uniform shirt and used it to try to put out the remaining flames.

Scottie backed away, swallowing a scream, and promptly began to choke.

Dani grabbed the radio personality's arm and dragged her down the steps and away from the patio. She dug through her belongings and thrust a bottle of water at the coughing woman.

A few seconds later, a fire engine and ambulance screeched to a stop in front of the building. They immediately took over from Spencer, moving him, Dani, and Scottie outside the perimeter they quickly established.

While a pair of EMTs took care of Scottie and the man with the cuts, Spencer retrieved his phone from

Dani and began making calls. She could hear him reporting to his boss, one of the university vice presidents, then phoning, and Wallace Zorillo. Finally, he began contacting his security team.

Several minutes later a second pair of EMTs were summoned to the patio. Dani's view was obstructed, but it was clear from the snatches of conversation she heard and the body language of the paramedics, that the figure on the ground was dead.

The police arrived next. Dani watched a guy in a suit, presumably the lead detective, step aside and speak into his car radio. She guessed he was calling the county coroner and the crime scene technicians.

A quick glance at her watch told Dani that it was nearly six thirty. Other contestants had been trickling into the area for the past half hour and everyone wanted to know what was going on.

Dani rose from where she had been sitting on the grass and walked over to Spencer, who had separated himself from the group. Having given up his uniform shirt, he was down to a white T-shirt.

She was about to ask if he was cold but knew he'd deny it even if he was, so instead she asked, "Did Mr. Zorillo say anything about what we should do?"

"He's arranging for you all to use the facilities that were set up in case of rain." Spencer frowned, clearly not in agreement with the plan. "When the union opens at seven, the contestants will be escorted into the large ballroom. Zorillo is sending his employees to gather the ingredients on the contestants' official list."

"So, the Chili Challenge is going on," Dani murmured thoughtfully.

"Against my advice." Spencer shook his head. "At least it will be easier to curtail access inside."

"Any news on Elvis?"

Spencer frowned. "According to local authorities, he's not at home and no one has seen him in that area."

"Shoot." Dani winced. "Any chance the person who was burned up was Elvis?"

Shaking his head, Spencer said, "Probably not. The body seemed a lot less bulky."

"Do you think the text Elvis sent me was genuine? I just realized that I have no idea how he got my cell number."

"Probably from the Chef-to-Go website." Spencer narrowed his eyes. "You really need to get a separate phone for the business."

"Possibly," Dani hedged, seeing no need for another expense.

Spencer put an arm around her shoulders. "How are you holding up? Do you want to drop out of the contest?"

"No, I can do it." Dani gazed into the warm depths of Spencer's eyes and immediately calmed down. "Shall I inform the other contestants of the new plan?"

Spencer nodded and, when his phone chirped, Dani waved and started toward where her fellow competitors where gathered. She paused before reaching them to watch a van drive up and park at the patio. It had MCCLEAN COUNTY CORONER painted in black with gold edging along its side, along with an insignia featuring a caduceus overlapped by the scales of justice.

A petite woman wearing a blue jumpsuit with DEPUTY CORONER stenciled across the back hopped out of the vehicle. She was followed by a large man in a similar one-piece garment, but with ASSISTANT CORONER printed on his uniform. He was pushing a metal gurney with a huge red duffel sitting on top of the shiny black bag spread out on the gurney's thin padding.

A shrill wail drew Dani's attention and she saw that the contestants were all gathered around Jade Lawrence, who was slumped on a bench. A gray wool blanket was around her shoulders, but she still shivered as she stared at the gurney.

Dani hadn't really gotten to know the woman,

but in observing her yesterday, she had appeared to be very fond of the limelight. And if her husband wasn't around, Dani had fully expected her to demand on-air time with Scottie that morning.

Tory Mays sat next to Jade, patting her hand and murmuring soothing words. When Dani approached, Tory got up.

She took a few steps away from Jade and said, "I saw you talking to the campus security chief. Does he know who's dead or what happened?"

"As far as I know, the body hasn't been identified." Dani answered. "And no one knows for sure what happened. But the contest is going on. At seven, we'll be escorted into the ballroom to the alternate cooking stations that were set up in case of bad weather. Everything we need will be provided."

Jill VanAsden had followed Tory and now touched her tote bag and said, "I'm glad I didn't leave my secret ingredient here overnight."

Dani ignored Jill's self-centered comment. "What happened to Jade?"

"All I can figure out is that around five this morning she told her husband she wanted to take a walk to clear her head and left him in bed. He was supposed to meet her here at six, and he isn't here."

Dani nodded, pretty sure that the life coach had intended to get herself interviewed by Scottie when the radio personality showed up to talk to Dani.

Jill continued, "Jade let out a scream when the coroner arrived, and she's been whimpering and rocking back and forth ever since. She hasn't said anything more." Tory bit her lip and lowered her voice. "I'm guessing she might think the person who died was him."

"Has anyone informed the police?" Dani looked around to see if she could spot the detective.

Tory shook her head. "Jade hasn't really said anything, and I didn't think it was my place."

"Okay. Let me tell Spencer and he can talk to the detective." She paused. "And we probably should have an EMT look over Jade."

Tory's fingers twisted in a knot. "If you think that's best."

"I don't know." Dani squatted in front of the life coach and studied her closely. Her breath was coming in small fast gasps, her skin was blotchy, and the area around her mouth had a bluish cast. Dani considered the symptoms, then said, "It looks like she's going into shock. We better get her help before we have a second body."

Chapter 15

Once Spencer called another ambulance for Jade and went off to talk to the police detective about her missing husband, Dani tuned out her fellow competitors' voices and focused on the life coach. "Jade, try and relax." She pressed her back so that she was lying on the bench, then elevated her feet by putting them on her tote bag. She kept her voice at a hypnotic tone as she loosened the shoelaces of the woman's athletic shoes. "Think of your favorite place."

Jade didn't respond. She appeared nearly catatonic.

Dani pulled the blanket higher around the woman's shoulders. She had done everything she could think of for Jade, and it was a relief when she heard an ambulance siren getting closer.

In minutes, a man and woman rushed over to them and began issuing orders and firing questions at her. Most of which she couldn't answer.

As Jade was being wheeled away, she suddenly became alert, grabbed Dani's hand, and begged, "Please, find Eli. I called his cell and he isn't answering."

She was saved from responding when the EMTs lifted the gurney into the ambulance. Dani had no idea where to look for Jade's husband. The best she could do was pass on the information about him being missing to Spencer.

While she had been with Jade, the county crime scene officers had arrived, and the patio was buzzing with voices and activity. Circling the crime scene, Dani made her way over to where Spencer was talking to the detective.

She caught Spencer's eye, then raised an eyebrow. Should she join them or wait somewhere else? He nodded And held his hand out to her.

When Dani reached his side, Spencer introduced her. "This is Detective Taylor. Ms. Sloan is my girlfriend, as well as one of the contestants. She and I arrived together this morning and were approaching the patio when the explosion occurred."

The detective nodded and asked, "Can you tell me your experience from the time you arrived in the parking lot until the fire department arrived?"

"Sure."

He took out a notepad and pen and motioned her to begin.

"Well, I gathered my things, got out of the truck, and started walking." Dani stopped and half closed her eyes. "Spencer was talking on his phone and was a little behind me when a guy rushed around the building and knocked my cup out of my hand."

Detective Taylor spoke up before Dani could say more. "What did this man look like?"

"He was about Spencer's height, but sort of beefy. He was wearing a custodian's coverall with the university insignia on it, a baseball cap, and sunglasses. I didn't see much of his face." Dani paused to gather her thoughts. "I got the impression he was in his thirties. But I don't know why I think that."

"You're doing great." Detective Taylor smiled. "Could you tell his race?"

Dani's brow creased as she tried to remember the details. "White. I saw the lower part of his face."

The detective asked a few more questions, then handed her his card and said, "Thank you for your cooperation."

He shook Dani and Spencer's hands, then went over to the patio and spoke to one of the firefighters.

As soon as he was out of sight, Dani asked, "When do you think they'll know who was killed?"

"I have no idea." He sighed. "I've got a call into the police chief, but she probably won't return it for several hours. Unless she was informed about this incident, I doubt she normally gets into her office much before eight and my message won't be a priority for her."

Dani nodded. "With Jade and Elvis gone, we're down to six contestants."

"Zorillo should just cancel."

"Does he know about Jade and her missing husband?"

"I filled in him earlier. Right after I told the detective."

"And?"

Spencer gritted his teeth. "He says the show must go on."

"Did the firefighters or Detective Taylor share anything?"

Crossing his arms, Spencer said, "First impressions are that the propone tank that was attached to the stove in the end cooking station exploded."

"So, it was an accident?"

He shook his head. "That's unlikely. According to the fire chief, the valve would have had to somehow come open, which would then cause a leak, and then the gas would have had to be exposed to a flame."

"Which means they're treating this as arson?"

Spencer nodded. "There are several possible scenarios. The person who was burned to death could be the one who loosened the valve and lit the fire. Or he was in the wrong place at the wrong time. Or the whole incident was aimed at killing him."

"Wait!" Dani held up her hand. "Didn't you say that you had one of your people guarding the patio? Could he or she have been the victim?"

"Thankfully no." Spencer frowned. "Evidently, at some point Douglas got bored spending the night watching an empty patio, decided being a campus security officer was not for him, and went home. He called the campus security number about an hour ago and left a message saying he quit. The dispatcher just passed it on to me a few minutes ago."

Dani rolled her eyes. "But he didn't inform anyone he had left his post last night?"

"No, that would have been too much trouble." Spencer sighed. "He had good recommendations, but when I asked him why he was changing jobs, he didn't really have a solid answer. I should have been suspicious when he said that he'd heard good things about Normalton and wanted to live here."

Before she could respond, Mavis rushed up and announced, "They're letting the contestants in now. We'd like you all to check your supplies and make sure there's nothing you need that's been overlooked."

"I'll be right there." Dani turned back to Spencer. "Let me know if you find out the victim's identity."

Spencer squeezed her hand. "Will do." She could feel his reluctance to let her go, but when he did, he said, "Be careful."

"Right." Dani took a step away, then turned back and said, "You be careful too. And text me if you find out anything."

With that, Dani hurried to catch up with Mavis and the other contestants, but skidded to a stop. *Shoot!* She'd left her box of equipment in the truck. She hoped no one took it.

Knowing she shouldn't go by herself, Dani scanned the area to see if anyone was available to accompany her, but everyone was busy. She paused, then shook her head. With all the first responders around, she was probably safer here than anywhere else.

Dani took one more look, then dug the tiny pepper spray out of the bottom of her purse and ran around the corner and toward the parking lot. As she reached the pickup, she noticed something a few feet away lying on the asphalt.

She stepped closer and nudged it with the toe of her shoe. It spread out and Dani realized she was staring at a discarded custodian's coverall. A baseball cap and a pair of sunglasses were also in the pile.

It looked just like what the guy who had bumped into her was wearing. This had to be a clue.

She'd better let the crime techs get it, but did she dare leave it? What if it someone took it?

Reaching into her pocket, she retrieved Detective Taylor's business card. Thankfully, her cell phone was fully charged.

Ten minutes later, a white panel truck with CRIME SCENE INVESTIGATOR painted in gold pulled into the lot and Dani waved it over. She pointed out the coverall, cap, and sunglasses, then excused herself.

She hastily collected her box from the truck bed, hurried around the building, and rushed into the union. There was a line for the elevators, so she and couple of the others took the stairs.

By the time Dani reached the third floor, she was out of breath, but she needed to get to her cooking station. She'd already lost valuable time. She was a step behind her competitors, and it would be bad for business if she placed last in the contest.

Chapter 16

For the second straight morning, Dani woke at the appalling hour of four thirty to her cell phone alarm blaring. Once again, she hurried through her morning ablutions, but this time she gulped down a cup of scalding coffee — burning her tongue in the process — and didn't have time to thaw out muffins. Hunger added to her bad temper.

Yesterday, when she'd finally gotten to the ballroom to start her practice cook, Wallace Zorillo met her at the door. He'd explained that to be fair to Jade, who was still being examined in the local ER, they were postponing the Chili Challenge until the next day.

Practice would start at five thirty and the contest would start at nine. The winner would be announced at one, allowing everyone to begin their travels home at a reasonable hour.

Which was why she was standing in the cold wind waiting to be picked up by her father.

Spencer hadn't been available this morning but didn't want her driving herself. Dani knew there was no way she'd get any of her boarders up and alert enough to be behind the wheel of a car at five in the morning, so she'd called her dad.

He'd sounded happy to help, which made her glad she'd asked him. Maybe he truly was changing.

As far as Dani knew, the investigations into both the previous sabotage and the explosion weren't going well for either Spencer or the police. When she'd found Spencer to inform him that the contest was postponed, he was knee-deep in giving orders and lining up interviews with suspects.

Spencer had hastily driven her home, dropping her off with a quick kiss and a promise to text her if anything developed. Not exactly how she had expected to spend her Saturday.

Now, Sunday morning felt like déjà vu to Dani as she slid into the passenger side of her father's gray Lincoln, slumped back against the seat, and closed her eyes.

At least Jonas's good morning was subdued.

Dani opened one eye and returned his greeting.

Jonas drove a mile or so in silence, then said, "I'm sorry I got you mixed up in this contest. If you want to drop out, I'd understand."

"Thanks, but with all the security officers and cops around, I'm probably safer in the ballroom than my own house."

Jonas nodded. "True. And I can stick around if you want."

"That's not necessary."

"Well. I'll be back at one to cheer when you win."

Dani forced a smile. "Or console me when I lose."

"Nonsense!" Jonas's head jerked toward Dani. "You can't think like that. You have to believe you're a champion."

"Right." Dani barely stopped herself from rolling her eyes. Evidently, her father had forgotten that until recently he'd made it clear that he thought she was anything but a winner.

"You are." Jonas scowled. "I'm sorry it took me so long to figure that out."

Dani swallowed a lump in her throat. "Thanks, Dad."

They were quiet until they pulled into the campus parking lot, then as he shut off the car's engine, Jonas asked, "Do you think any of the contestants will drop out?"

"Only the one that already left." Dani stepped from the MKZ.

Jonas plucked the box from Dani's arms. "I'll carry this upstairs for you."

"Thanks." Dani hurried toward the union's entrance where she greeted the security guard on duty and showed him her ID and vouched for her father.

Once they made it through the lobby, up the elevator, and into the ballroom, Jonas put Dani's carton on the counter at her station and looked around. "It appears that we're the first ones here. I'll stick around until the others show up."

Before she could respond, Dani heard the door open and a familiar voice yelled, "Howdy!"

It couldn't be. Slowly, she turned her head and looked behind her. Walking down the aisle, wearing a powder blue jumpsuit, was the missing competitor. Elvis had returned.

He grabbed Dani in a hug. "I bet you weren't expecting me."

Jonas thundered, "Get your hands off my daughter!"

"It's all right, Dad." Dani wiggled free and crossed her arms. "This is Elvis. The contestant from Missouri."

Narrowing his eyes, Jonas said, "I thought he quit."

"So did I." She turned to Elvis. "What happened?"

"Well, the closer I got to home, the more I felt like a durned coward. So, I turned around and drove back." Elvis frowned. "But when I got here, I heard about the explosion and the contest being postponed, so I let old Wallace know that I was back, then checked into the Mercury Inn. I figured that I couldn't be the next victim if no one but him knew I was here."

"That's great." Dani edged away. "I guess we'd better get to work."

Once Dani reached her station, she put Elvis out of her mind, and began to assemble the ingredients for her recipe. While she worked, the remaining contestants began to arrive. Everyone wore the same determined look.

This was the day. Either they'd take home one of the three prizes, or they'd leave with nothing.

As the ballroom started to fill with the sounds and smells of food being prepared, Dani stirred her ground turkey. It was just beginning to break into crumbles. Diced green pepper, onions, and sweet potatoes went in next, followed by minced garlic.

While the mixture was browning, Dani looked over her competition. Jade seemed as perky as ever, so it appeared the burned corpse hadn't been her husband after all.

Pushing aside her concern for the poor victim, Dani transferred the meat and vegetables, carefully including the drippings, into a large pot. She covered it with plastic wrap, then got out her smoke gun.

Once the gun was filled with apple chips, she inserted the rubber tube under the cellophane and turned on the power switch. She held it there for three minutes then allowed the mixture to rest for an additional three minutes before adding tomato sauce and diced tomatoes.

Dani had brought both of those items with her. She'd preserved them from her summer garden, and nothing tasted like homegrown tomatoes.

The green chili peppers were from the supermarket, but she'd ground the ancho chili powder from poblano peppers she'd grown, then smoked and dried. She'd also made her own peanut butter. Salt and paprika were the last ingredients to go into the pan.

Turning the flame to low, Dani decided to visit her competition and see what everyone was saying about the explosion.

Spencer hadn't exactly suggested that she investigate, but he had told her to keep her ears open. And she wouldn't be able to hear anything unless she wandered around.

While she couldn't take notes as she chatted, she did have a small spiral pad in the pocket of the new apron she'd been issued. If someone said something relevant, she could always duck into the restroom and jot it down.

Best case scenario, she would overhear conversations, but with them all so spread out, she'd probably have to prime the pump. Having worked in HR for so many years, she was pretty good at getting people to talk.

The first station that Dani approached belonged to Tory Mays. The yoga instructor was frowning at a can of pinto beans and muttering about it being the wrong kind.

"Hi!" Dani leaned against the table serving as Tory's front counter. "How are you holding up after yesterday?"

Tory put down the can and picked up a bottle of barbecue sauce. "Okay, I guess. But I sure wish I would have brought more of my own ingredients. I'm not familiar with these brands."

"That must be hard." Dani fought the urge to be selfish, but gave up and said, "I believe they're buying all our stuff from the three big grocery stores, but there are quite a few specialties food markets in town. Maybe you could request they try one of them."

Tory tilted her head. "That's a good idea. Thanks."

"Have you heard anything about the explosion or who was killed?"

Leaning forward across the counter, Tory lowered her voice. "Not much. Everyone was talking about it, but no one had any real news."

"Yeah. I'm guessing the authorities will keep most of the details pretty quiet."

Tory straightened. "Oh. I did hear that Jade's husband turned up safe and sound. Turns out he went for a swim in the union's indoor pool and lost track of time."

"What a relief." Dani fanned her hand in front of her face. "Jade had to be ecstatic."

Moving back to her stove, Tory said over her shoulder, "You'd think so, wouldn't you?

"She wasn't?"

Tory shrugged. "Maybe. Who knows?"

Dani wished Tory luck, then moved on to Ruben Caballero. He was waving a wooden spoon and talking to Scottie Diller. He wore jeans, a plaid shirt, red suspenders, and an annoyed expression.

Ruben's booming baritone echoed off the ballroom walls. "If you say anything to Mr. Zorillo, I'll sue you for slander."

Dani stopped just out of sight. She wanted to know what he was talking about, but not enough to get involved.

"All I said was that I heard you arguing with some guy Friday." Scottie Diller crossed her arms. "Just tell me who he was, and once I talk to him to make sure he's not the person who was killed in the fire, I'll let it go."

Ruben glared. "It's none of your damn business so butt out."

Dani looked at her watch. She rushed back to her station, adjusted the flame under her pot and gave the contents a stir. Tasting the chili, she smacked her lips, then added her last ingredient, cocoa powder.

That done, she headed to her right, where Jill VanAsden was working. The soccer mom was pouring what looked like a beer into her stockpot. When she noticed Dani, she quickly hid the bottle and glared at her.

"Hi!" Dani pasted a smile on her face. "How's everything going?"

Jill continued to scowl. "Why do you ask?"

"Uh." Dani wasn't prepared for that response, and she stuttered, "I-it's j-just after what happened yesterday, I was w-wondering how we all were doing."

The soccer mom stared. "Why wouldn't I be fine? It's not as if what happened had anything to do with me."

"Well, technically maybe that's true, but it could have been a close call for any of us."

Jill crossed her arms. "Not me. The station that blew up wasn't even on my side of the space." She shot Dani a speculative look. "Yours either since you were right next to me."

"Oh, that's right." Dani nodded.

Jill pointedly turned away from Dani, clearly indicating the conversation was over.

Dani hadn't thought about the precise location of the explosion, however now that Jill mentioned it, the person who had been on fire was in front of Elvis's assigned spot. But Elvis was alive and well, so that didn't really help identify the victim.

Still, maybe it was time to have a talk with the disappearing grill master. It was a little suspicious that he'd left so mysteriously, then reappeared after the explosion.

Elvis's back was to Dani when she arrived at his station. He was holding a colander and lifting the lid to his pot.

"Hey—"

When Dani spoke, he threw up his hands, yelping in fright. The strainer slipped from his fingers, spilling its contents on the ground, and Elvis gasped for air.

Wow! Dani would have never pegged the grill master as so jumpy. Was he afraid he might be the next victim. Someone *had* nearly run him over after lunch.

Or was he on edge because he was the killer? His behavior had been a bit shady. He hadn't wanted to call the police and then he'd disappeared.

Dani hesitated. She'd have to be careful. If Elvis was the killer, she didn't want to paint a target on her back. And if he was the intended victim, she didn't want the killer to associate her with him.

Chapter 17

Spencer eyed the crowd milling around the ballroom. At nine o'clock, Wallace Zorillo had blown a whistle and the Chili Challenge had officially started. Each contestant had until noon to complete their dish. Bowls would go to the judges, to the photographer for pictures, and the rest would be put in taster-size paper cups for the audience to sample.

This many people in an uncontrolled environment made Spencer nervous. He had tried to persuade Zorillo to exclude spectators, but when the company president had refused to listen, Spencer had stationed one of his security team members between each of the kitchen setups. Every officer was responsible for two contestants and an additional guard was assigned to the judges.

Since Warren Douglas had quit without notice, the five men were all Spencer could spare. He had to keep the remaining two, Robert Porter and Lavonia Jools, patrolling the rest of the campus.

To make up for the lack of additional officers, Spencer planned to continually walk through the area watching for anyone that acted in a suspicious manner. If he passed by Dani's station more often than any of the others, it was pure coincidence.

As Spencer marched by Dani's space for the third time, she was preparing to smoke the meat and vegetable mixture that she had just placed in a large stockpot. The procedure had drawn a large audience and he slowed his pace to keep an eye on the crowd.

While his gaze skipped from face-to-face evaluating the threat level, Spencer ground his teeth. Chief Cleary hadn't returned his call, and with all the competitors, judges, and contest personnel accounted for, he had no name for the victim of the propane explosion.

In addition, the Taylors had confided that they didn't have any witnesses to the incident. The union security cameras had only caught the back of a blurry figure loitering near the kitchen setup on the patio. For all they knew that person might have been Douglas patrolling the area before he decided to walk off the job.

Until the ME made an identification, the police had little to go on. Spencer was reduced to tracking down the campus activist leaders who had been unhappy with the Route 66 Rally. And so far, three of the four had airtight alibis for the explosion, if not the other sabotage.

Spencer refocused on Dani as she finished with the smoke gun and began to add the additional ingredients that she had lined up on the table. With her activity becoming less interesting, the onlookers began to drift away.

Now that the people in front of her had dispersed, Dani waved at Spencer and asked, "How's it going?"

"So far, so good." Spencer smiled. "Do you need anything?"

Dani shook her head. "Thanks. Once I get this simmering, I'll grab something to eat, but I can wait until then."

"Okay. I'd better get back to work." Spencer started to leave, but paused and said, "Be careful. Text me if anything makes you uncomfortable."

Dani didn't look up from her cooking. "Will do."

Spencer hated to leave her alone, but duty called. The contestants would be in full view and thus safe from any sneak attacks, so he headed over to the hospitality lounge—a walled-off section furnished with tables and chairs. Coffee, tea, and soft drinks were provided, along with small pastries and sandwiches.

The three judges sat at a table against the back wall, deeply involved in a conversation. Spencer edged closer and grabbed a can of Dr Pepper. He took his time opening it and pouring it into a cup, hoping to overhear what they were saying.

He concentrated on being inconspicuous, silently choosing a bear claw. Careful not to make eye contact, he selected a seat off to the side. He wasn't facing them, but he could still see them. Someone had left the Sports Section of the Normalton paper on the table, and he opened it in front of his face, keeping it below eye level.

As he hoped, the judges paid no attention to him and continued their discussion.

The first thing Spencer heard was Hugh Granville chuckle. "I doubt they'll ever figure out who bumped off that crispy critter. The coppers here are straight out of *The Simpsons*. Chief Wiggum questioned me yesterday and could barely spell my name correctly."

"Why are you so happy about that?" Latoya Lin snapped. "Do you want someone to get away with murder?" The food critic looked over her glasses at the celebrity chef. "Or maybe you're the killer."

"You're lucky I'm not." Hugh raised his chin belligerently, then smirked. "It was probably one of those protesters."

Mick Owen wrinkled his brow. "What protestors? I haven't seen any protestors."

"The arse ringing my room every five minutes, whinging about cooking with our animal friends," Hugh growled. "Haven't you had any calls?"

Both Latoya and Mick said no, then Mick asked, "Who do you think was the victim?"

"That's the question, isn't it?" Latoya fingered her napkin. "All the contest people seem to be accounted for."

Mick shook his head. "The poor guy who died was probably some random person who just wanted to get a closer look at the setup."

"Or," Hugh raised an eyebrow, "maybe it was some daft bloke mucking about with the equipment and managed to off himself."

Latoya tapped her fingers on the tabletop. "You know. It could be someone connected with the company sponsoring the contest."

"Why do you say that?" Mick asked.

Lowering her voice, Latoya said, "UFE is in trouble. They're being pressured to stop doing business with China and live up to their name by using American companies as their suppliers. The last thing they need is more bad press."

Spencer blinked. He hadn't heard anything about the company having problems. When he'd questioned Zorillo about anyone wanting to harm him or his business, the company president had vehemently denied the idea that he or UFE could possibly be the target.

Spencer rose from his seat, threw away his trash

and marched out of the lounge area. It was time to have another conversation with Zorillo. And this time the man would give him some real answers instead of the corporate BS he'd been handing out.

Chapter 18

When Spencer had stopped by, Dani had been busy and forgotten to tell Spencer about Elvis's skittish behavior. As soon as she finished what she'd been doing, she went in search of him, but he'd been nowhere to be found.

Giving up, she retrieved her watch from her apron pocket, checked the time, and frowned.

Shoot! She'd been gone longer than she planned. She needed to stir her chili and add the secret ingredient.

Hurrying back to her workspace, she prayed it wasn't too late for the cocoa powder to add the flavor she hoped to achieve. Or even worse, that the chili had stuck to the pot.

After dashing behind the table, Dani grabbed a wooden spatula, raised the lid, and cautiously scraped it along the bottom of the pan. When it didn't encounter any resistance, she let out a sigh of relief. It hadn't burned.

Her chili smelled wonderful and when she carefully added the cocoa powder, the aroma was even better. Now she just had to let it simmer until Mr. Zorillo called time.

As she turned from the stove, a familiar voice asked, "Have you heard anything about the person who was killed in the explosion?"

Dani rested a hip on the counter and raised a brow at her boarder Tippi Epstein. "According to Spencer, the police haven't identified the body yet. Why are you interested?"

"Well." The tiny brunette smoothed her sleek bob. "If it turns out to be something interesting, I might use the case for my Public Speaking class. The prof is giving the person with the best speech an automatic A for the semester."

Dani nodded. She wasn't surprised. The young woman didn't allow emotion to sidetrack her from her goal of getting into an Ivy League law school.

"I'll let you know when I find out the name of the victim." Dani took a seat on one of the two folding chairs at her station.

Tippi leaned down and stared into Dani's eyes. "Promise?"

"Girl Scout's honor." Dani smiled and held up the three middle fingers of her right hand. Then she frowned and asked, "Anything new at home?" This past week she'd been so tied up in the Chili Challenge she'd lost touch with what was going on with her friends. "Everyone okay?"

A couple of years ago, heck eighteen months

ago, Dani had had very few people in her life to worry about. But now her circle was bursting. There were the three college girls, Ivy, Tippi, and Starr, who lived in the mansion with her. Plus, Atti and her dog Khan who lived in the studio apartment in the carriage house. Not to mention Frannie and Justin who, even when no story was brewing, had seemed to hang around a lot, and now were living in one of the two-bedroom carriage house apartments.

Dani refocused just in time to hear Tippi say, "Ivy and Laz have been spending most of their time at the library. They both have big exams coming up. Starr is doing everything but sleeping in the genetics lab. And I have no idea what Little Orphan Atti is up to today, but she begged me to check in here to make sure you were okay."

"I've asked you to not call her that." Dani crossed her arms. Tippi hadn't been a fan of Dani allowing Atti to live in the carriage house apartment in exchange for work hours. She, and the previously homeless girl, had not clicked and both tended to avoid each other. "It makes me very uncomfortable."

Tippi shrugged. "Then please cancel my subscription to your issues."

"That kind of snarkiness is offensive." Dani refused to backdown.

Tippi raised both brows. "If you're offended by

the things I say, imagine the stuff that I hold back."

"Acting like that doesn't make you seem smart or cool."

Tippi chewed on her bottom lip, then twitched her shoulders and said, "I just call them like I see them."

"A closed mouth gathers no foot." Dani maintained eye contact until Tippi looked away.

"Fine." Tippi huffed, then tossed her head. "Well, if there's nothing new about Charcoal Charlie, I guess, I'll go find Caleb. His study group is meeting in one of the rooms downstairs and it should be almost over. He can take me out for some ice cream."

Tippi left before Dani could chide her about using such an insensitive nickname for the explosion victim. Dani made a mental note to sit down with Tippi when she had more time. She needed to find a way to persuade her to be less cruel toward others.

Sighing, Dani pushed aside her concerns and stood up. She stirred the chili. It looked good. She took a disposable spoon from the package and dipped it into the bubbling mixture.

Once it cooled off a bit, she slipped the utensil into her mouth and thoughtfully chewed. Surprised, she took another spoon from the box and tasted another bite.

It was good! In fact, it was the best batch she'd

ever managed to make. Maybe she had a chance to win after all.

Dani turned the flame under her pot even lower, then checked her watch. She had nearly half an hour until the contest ended. Who hadn't she looked in on?

There were so many people involved, it was hard to keep them straight. She'd definitely seen Elvis. She'd spoken to Jill and Tory, and witnessed Ruben's fight with Scottie —

Oops!

She dug out her cell and fired off a text to Spencer regarding what the radio personality had said about Ruben's argument with an unknown man. And while she was at it, she added her thoughts about Elvis being the possible intended victim.

Who did that leave? *Jade!*

Dani bit her lip. She really should check in on the nutritionist. Maybe, when she'd been transported to the hospital, she'd overheard something from the first responders.

Making her way through the packed aisles toward Jade's area, Dani abruptly stopped and frowned. Why did she keep forgetting about the engineer from Texas and the lawyer from Oklahoma?

Heck! She couldn't even remember their names. In mystery novels the people who were the most invisible were always the killers. Maybe she should track those two contestants down first.

Dani tapped her foot. Alphabetically, their states were the last two represented so their stations should be next to each other near the exit.

Wiggling her way through the crowd, she finally found the pair. Once she saw them, she remembered that the engineer went by JM and the lawyer was named Milton. Both appeared hard at work on their chili.

Dani greeted JM who barely glanced up as he said hi. It was clear he wasn't open to chatting.

Milton was even worse. When she spoke to him, he looked at her for a long second, then curled his lip and silently returned to what he'd been doing.

Blowing a strand of hair out of her eyes, Dani gave up. She'd use the time that she had left to talk to Jade.

But again, she halted. Realistically, she wasn't sure ten minutes was enough to find out anything. It would probably be better to finish her chili, then investigate.

As she put the final touches on her recipe, Dani daydreamed about what she would do with the prize money. Most of it would have to be earmarked for the loan she'd taken out to remodel the carriage house, but she would use a little for some new clothes. Now that she and Spencer were seeing so much of each other, she couldn't just wear the same thing over and over again.

A few moments later, Dani delivered the chili to Mavis who would oversee the distribution to the photographers, judges, and spectators. Free of her obligations, she sought out Jade. Surprisingly, when she arrived at the nutritionist's workstation, a group was gathered around it.

Dani squirmed her way to the front of the mob and saw that Jade was still cooking. Her husband was standing a few steps behind her holding a spoon as if it were a scalpel ready to be slapped into a surgeon's waiting hand.

Checking her watch, Dani held her breath. Jade had only two minutes to get her chili in the bowls and the bowls to the judges.

This was not the time to attempt to have a casual conversation.

Chapter 19

For the first time that day, Dani was at a loss as what to do with her time. Talking with Jade would have to wait until the woman was done with her chili and had presented it to the contest officials. Milton and JM had made it clear they weren't the chatty type.

It would be a good hour or more until the winner was announced. Who else could she probe for clues?

Dani was standing near the rear of the ballroom, trying to come up with a plan, when she heard a commotion over in the corner.

Two male voices battled to be heard, but a loud alto drowned them all out. "I'm gonna pop both of you upside the head if you don't calm down."

Dani edged closer. Once she got within a few feet, she could see Lavonia Jools, an ex-MP and one of Spencer's security team. She was between a brawny young man with bright red hair and Hugh Granville. The young guy was massaging his chin and the judge held a hand over his left eye.

Hmm! Dani scratched her head. Where had she seen the redhead before? And hadn't Spencer mentioned that Lavonia was on campus patrol?

Before Dani could come up with any answers, she saw the security guard had a grip on both men's upper arms. The woman looked as if what she really wanted to do was shake them both like a dust mop but was holding on to her temper by sheer willpower.

Hugh Granville shouted, "This muppet assaulted me!"

"I only hit him after he punched me," the redhead protested still nursing his jaw.

"Why would he do that?" Lavonia let go of the men and crossed her arms.

The younger man puffed out his chest. "I told him that he was a mass murderer."

Dani gasped softly. Had the redhead seen the TV chef messing with the propane tank?

"And, after I got this…this inane *vegan's* attention with a little tap to his chin, I explained that scientific studies prove eating meat comes naturally, and animal protein is how we became verbal and more intelligent." Hugh smirked.

"L-liar!" The redhead stuttered. "You punched me hard and there's no way that study is right." He paused, then added, "And I'm proud to be a vegan."

Lavonia narrowed her eyes. "Okay, Mister…?"

"Hamilton Butcher," the redhead supplied, then shot a look of loathing at Hugh when he burst out laughing.

"You, Mr. Butcher," Lavonia continued, "and you, Mr. Granville, have a difference of opinion."

"It's more than an opinion," Hamilton objected. "We have to stop killing and eating our animal brethren."

"Never going to happen, mate. If we weren't meant to eat animals, why are they made of meat?" Hugh snorted so hard he must have hurt himself because he rubbed his chest.

Hamilton pointed at the judge's hand as it massaged his breastbone and crowed. "Just remember, heart attacks are God's revenge for eating his animal friends."

"Right." Lavonia rolled her eyes and took Hamilton's arm. "Neither of you is going to change the other's mind, so let's call this a draw. You are now banned from the ballroom until this contest is over." She then zeroed in on the TV chef. "And shouldn't you be with the other judges doing judgy things?"

While both men muttered their displeasure, neither appeared to want to get on the security guard's bad side by saying anything directly to her. And although Hamilton dragged his feet, Lavonia didn't seem to have any problems compelling him toward the exit.

Hugh maintained his position while waving at

the departing vegan and taunting him by yelling, "Bye-bye, you knob."

"Where have you been?" Amelia rushed up to Hugh. "They're waiting for you at the judges table."

"Let them."

Amelia started tugging on his arm. "The sooner you do this, the sooner you can fly back to California."

"Finally," Hugh huffed. "But next time the producers insist on my traveling to some backwater, I'm sending a stunt double."

Dani shook her head. She felt sorry for the chef's assistant. How did she put up with that jerk?

Still, she'd bet her best knife that Amelia had the upper hand in that relationship. Dani couldn't put her finger on it, but there was something about that woman that just cried out power.

Although Lavonia would probably inform Spencer of what was going on, Dani thought it might be a good idea to track him down and let him know there'd been a raging vegan in the ballroom.

Wouldn't somebody as militant as Hamilton Butcher be a likely suspect in fiddling with the propane tank of a cooking contest using lots of meat? He may not even have intended to harm anyone, just cause the competition to be cancelled.

Now where would Spencer be? Dani started

down the nearest aisle. She'd just walk up and down the rows until she found him.

As she made her way through the observers, she scanned back and forth for any sign of Spencer, but he was nowhere to be seen. Maybe she should just text him.

However, before she got out her phone, she ran into another altercation. A crowd had formed a semicircle around a man dressed in jeans and a plaid flannel shirt with a long black braid over his shoulder. He was tall and broad, and easily held a much smaller security guard in what was clearly an unreturned hug.

The guard, who looked a lot like Barney Fife from that old television program, was squirming and yelling, "Leave me go! I ain't that kind of dude!"

Edging her way through the mob, Dani tried to come up with something to say, but as she emerged from the throng all she could think of was, "Unhand that man this instant."

Dani snorted silently. She sounded like some Victorian dowager.

Mr. Braid looked through Dani as if she hadn't spoken, then turned his attention back to the guard. "As a representative of the Peace and Love Network, I, Quest Lightfoot, declare this competition inhumane. There will be no individual winners. All contestants are equals."

Dani hated being ignored. It had happened far too often in her previous profession in the Human Relations field. Her suggestions went unheeded until her bosses found themselves served with papers for a lawsuit, and then they blamed her for the problem they themselves had created.

How could she get through to this person? Maybe Dani should sound her emergency whistle. Barney was being touched inappropriately and without his consent, surely that qualified as an urgent situation.

But before Dani could figure out if a hug counted as sexual assault, the guard wiggled out of Lightfoot's grasp.

Spittle flew from his mouth as he yelled, "I keep telling you, I don't have nothing to do with how the contest is run!"

Lightfoot made a grab for Barney but missed. "Then I'll just have to shut this thing down some other way."

Oh, no. Dani tensed. Was this the saboteur? If so, what was he planning on blowing up next?

While Dani was fumbling with her cell phone, trying to decide if she should call Spencer first or just go ahead and dial 911, Detective Taylor materialized next to Lightfoot.

Where did he come from?

Taylor's hand rested on a Taser clipped to his belt and he maneuvered the security guard out of hugging range. The detective wore a wrinkled gray suit and the bags under his eyes were big enough to qualify as checked luggage on an airplane.

A movement behind Lightfoot dragged Dani's gaze from the detective. Sneaking up on the group were three other students wearing T-shirts that stated, Make love not chili.

Dani flinched. They were unarmed, but increased numbers could be a problem. As the group got closer, the stench of patchouli mixed with the body odor that surrounded the trio created an olfactory nightmare.

While Dani had been distracted by the Peace and Love Network crew, Hamilton Butcher had somehow snuck back into the ballroom and now he flanked Detective Taylor. The vegan was dressed as a pig and unfolded a sign that read My blood is on your hands. He seemed unaware of the irony of his choice of costume with a name like his.

Dani knew she had to do something before some actual plasma was shed. The mood among the crowd watching the protesters was getting ugly and the audience was closing in on the activists. The spectators were probably all meat eaters and were there to see who won the contest, not declare it a draw.

Desperate, Dani took out her whistle, drew in a big breath, and blew.

Chapter 20

Dani wasn't sure if it was the shrill whistle or if the student activists finally noticed they were playing to a hostile audience, but the swine, the hugger, and the make-love-not-chili trio all turned away from the detective and were now focused on Dani.

"Are you in charge of the contest?" Hamilton pointed his hoof at her.

"No." Dani took a few steps back, hoping to see Spencer hurrying towards her. "Wallace Zorillo represents the company sponsoring this event."

"Where is he?" Hamilton demanded.

All eyes swung toward her, and she quickly said, "No idea."

"Really?" The vegan glared at her as if she were concealing the man under her apron and Dani cringed. Ignorance was clearly not an acceptable excuse.

As if to prove Dani's thoughts correct, one of the peaceniks pointed his sign at her and said, "I bet you're hiding him. You're one of the contestants, aren't you?"

"No." Dani gulped. "I mean yes, I'm competing in the challenge, but I haven't seen Mr. Zorillo in hours."

Quest Lightfoot had moved so close to Dani she could see the pores on his nose when he shouted, "Shouldn't he be here, strutting around encouraging people to compete rather than cooperate? You're protecting him, aren't you?"

His fellow protestors all moved closer until Dani felt as if she were going to be crushed by them.

Great, she was about to be torn apart by an activist mob at a cooking contest because she had tried to prevent them from ganging up on the security guard and the detective. Speaking of Taylor, why wasn't he helping her?

She scanned the area until she saw him. He was nearby and still had his hand on his Taser, but he seemed content to let the situation play out without interfering.

Dani swallowed — her throat had gone dry — then raised her voice and tried to placate the students. "Your concerns have been noted by everyone here, and I'm sure the journalists present will report your protests in the newspapers, on the radio, and on social media. Getting your point out to millions is really more of a win than stopping the contest would be."

As if to prove her point, a flash went off behind her. Dani whirled around. Reporters were taking notes, photographers were clicking cameras, and Scottie Diller was rushing forward with her microphone at the ready.

Fleetingly, Dani considered attempting a quick getaway. But since several flashes had already gone off and Scottie had been recording for who knows how long, there was no point in leaving.

Besides, someone should try to do something to mitigate the damage. Mr. Zorillo and his company had just been trying to do something positive for the community, and this type of media exposure couldn't be good for their brand. Where were the business's PR people? Surely, they could handle the situation.

Dani scanned the crowd, then narrowed her eyes. Was that Mr. Zorillo's executive assistant standing just beyond the media doing nothing?

Yes, it was.

Dani led the crowd toward him, and when she could speak without having to shout, she said, "Bert, you need to do something."

Frowning, he asked, "What happened?"

Dani explained the protestors, ending with, "You should make a statement."

Bert bit his thumbnail. "I'd better fetch Mr. Zorillo."

He was still trying to get a signal on his cell phone when a gunshot rang out through the ballroom. Instinctively, Dani tackled the young man. Bert and Dani flew backwards, taking out a cluster of bystanders as if they were bowling pins. It was a perfect strike and they all ended up on the floor in an ungainly heap.

A few seconds later, having somehow ended up on the bottom of the pile, Dani worked to free herself from the tangle of arms and legs. Once her head was clear of the pileup, she heard more screams and shouting. Her first clear view was of running feet and a panicked crowd.

Only the thought of being crushed as the mob grew, motivated her to continue freeing herself rather than pulling Bert back over her like a blanket. And even then, it took Dani several minutes to persuade Bert to get off her as he was reluctant to stand up. He kept repeating that the floor was the safest place if there was going to be more shooting.

The situation *was* precarious, and she could hardly blame him for being a bit disinclined to rise to the occasion. Although there hadn't been any more gunshots, the spectators were still charging toward the exit like Black Friday shoppers intent on the single, one-hundred-dollar computer available. They were mowing down anyone and anything in their path.

Finally, with one last mighty pull, Dani heaved

Bert to his feet and looked around. Not everyone had followed the herd, but the ballroom had thinned considerably, including all the protesters.

With fewer people, Dani could see Jill VanAsden standing near the judges' table holding a pistol in the air. The soccer mom had a determined look on her face.

She swept the area before tucking away the gun and declaring, "Now we can get on with the contest."

Detective Taylor shouted, "Put down your weapon!"

"I have a constitutional right to bear arms," Jill announced as she placed the gun on the floor. The detective moved forward and picked the weapon up.

After securing the gun, he handcuffed the soccer mom and escorted her out of the ballroom. They had barely cleared the exit when Spencer rushed inside.

He headed straight to his security guard, who was just now crawling out of his hidey-hole. He had evidently taken cover under an overturned table and remained there until he was good and sure it was safe to emerge.

When Spencer got to the guy, he demanded, "Jacobs, what in the holy hell is going on in here? I leave you alone for ten minutes and we have a riot?"

"Sir, the protestors came out of nowhere and I was outnumbered." The security guard held up a bright yellow object. "I was going to Taser them, but a lady started shooting and everyone ran."

While Spencer continued to question his guard, Bert gathered the Chili Challenge staff and worked on getting people refocused on the contest. Some were long gone, but many had lingered in the hallway.

With Spencer busy and the shooter removed, Dani decided her best option was to head to her workspace. She would wait there until summoned to hear the results.

Soon afterwards, Mr. Zorillo announced that Jill was disqualified, but the judging would continue. As far as Dani could see, the other contestants appeared to have either ignored the ruckus or taken a look and returned to their stations.

No one was talking, so Dani sank onto a chair and wondered what else could go wrong with this competition. As soon as the thought crossed her mind, she mentally slapped herself for putting that kind of challenge out to the universe.

Dani felt drained. There was nothing she could do now. The only bright spot was that in an hour or so, it all would be over.

Willing herself to get up off the chair, Dani started to rise just as her father rushed into the workspace. He skidded to a stop and stared at her, then grabbed her and wrapped her in his arms. He was gasping for air and seemed unable to form any words.

Closing his eyes, Jonas leaned his forehead against hers and panted, "I was never so scared in my life. I had been looking for you when I heard the gunshot, then everyone took off running. Someone said they saw you go down and I couldn't find you anywhere."

"I'm fine." Dani patted her father's back. "The bullet was nowhere near me."

Jonas took a calming breath. "Do you know what happened?"

Dani gave her dad a final pat before stepping out of his embrace. "It all started with a vengeful vegan."

Chapter 21

Dani had just said goodbye to her father, and he had left to get a good seat for the announcement of the Chili Challenge winner, when Jade bustled into Dani's cubicle. Her critical stare examined every inch of the workspace. She closed a slightly ajar cupboard door, then ran her finger over the stove's cook top.

Frowning, Dani opened her mouth to ask what in the heck the nutritionist thought she was doing, but before she could speak Jade announced, "I want to talk to you."

"Oh?"

Dani crossed her arms and waited. As it turned out, she wanted to talk to Jade too, so she was curious what the woman had to say.

Strangely, the nutritionist continued her inspection of Dani's cooking area. Was she getting her nerve up to start the conversation or just OCD?

Jade scraped something off the counter with her fingernail, flicked the debris in the wastebasket, then said, "You should really get rid of your garbage." She held up a white plastic sack closed with a yellow twist tie. "We can throw out mine and yours both on the way to the judging."

"Don't they have someone to do that?" Dani raised a brow at the women's peculiar behavior.

What was she up to?

Jade stared at Dani, then looked pointedly at the bin. "Do you really want some stranger going through your trash? That's how identities are stolen."

"I don't think they can find out much from my empty cans and bottles."

"Why take the chance?" Jade narrowed her eyes. "We should at least throw ours in the communal cans so that no one can tell which is ours versus what belongs to someone else."

Clearly the nutritionist was way more paranoid than Dani had realized. Studying the woman, she wondered if thinking that her husband was dead had affected her in a way that no one had realized. Maybe it was best to play along with her.

Pasting a smile on her face, Dani said, "Sure. Better safe than sorry." As she eased the garbage bag from the bin and tied it off, she said, "By the way, how are you feeling? That was a terrible scare you had yesterday."

"Fine." Jade put her left hand to her chest, the right one still clutching her garbage bag. "Once I saw Eli and knew he hadn't been the one killed by the explosion, it was all okay."

Dani nodded. "That must have been such a

relief. I imagine you don't even remember your ride to the hospital or what happened there."

Tilting her head encouragingly, Dani hoped Jade would take the bait.

"Well," the nutritionist pursed her lips, "I do recall bits and pieces. The paramedics apparently didn't realize that I thought the victim of the explosion was my husband because they were chattering on about how difficult it is to identify bodies that had been burned." Jade frowned. "They also said that the cops had lucked out since they had recovered some item that wasn't completely destroyed."

"Really?" Dani held her breath. "Did they say what it was?"

Jade shrugged. "A medal of some kind."

"How interesting." Before the nutritionist could respond, Dani asked, "Were the people at the hospital talking about the explosion?"

Jade twitched her shoulders. "Eli was waiting there for me, and I was so relieved that I didn't pay any attention to anyone but him after that."

"Of course." Dani nodded, picking up her bag of trash. "Well, I guess we should get up to the judging area."

"Wait!" Jade stepped in Dani's path. When she frowned, the nutritionist stuttered, "I-I mean, we have plenty of time and I was hoping you had some information about the explosion since your boyfriend is the head of security."

Dani moved slightly back, uncomfortable with the woman's invasion of her personal space. "Sadly, with all the problems the challenge has created, he's been so busy we haven't had a chance to talk much."

"Yes, this whole contest almost seems cursed, doesn't it?" Jade shuddered. "All the sabotage and the fatal explosion, then today's protests and near-riots. I wish I had never entered."

Dani patted Jade's shoulder, then nudged her to get her moving. The two of them walked out from the workspace and toward the rear of the room where a pair of enormous trash receptacles stood against the back wall.

As far as Dani could see, although the other competitors had all left their cubicles, the judges were still behind their table tasting and retasting the contestants' chili. The media hovered around the judges, making notes.

When they reached the huge green bins, Dani heaved her bag over the edge and Jade did the same. Then they headed toward the front of the ballroom where the announcement of the winner would take place.

When they reached the raised platform, the

chairs facing the judges were full. Luckily, there were seats for the contestants lined up on the dais.

Jade and Dani sank into their designated spots in silence. Dani was exhausted from cooking, as well as everything else that had gone on. She rested her head on the seatback and closed her eyes, not opening them until she felt Jade nudge her.

The nutritionist asked, "Why is this taking so long?"

"No idea," Dani said, then added, "Win, lose, or draw, I'll be glad to have this whole thing over with."

Jade lowered her voice. "Me too."

Dani spotted her father in the front row chatting with an attractive fifty-something woman. They seemed too friendly to have just met. Could she be the infamous Beverly her dad had been dating?

Waiting until she caught his eye, Dani waved at her father and inclined her head toward his companion. He returned her wave but ignored her questioning expression.

Dani scanned the rest of the spectators, hoping to see Spencer. Intellectually, she knew he was too busy to sit around waiting for the winner to be announced, but she was still a little disappointed.

Oh, well, at least her dad was there. Something that up until a few months ago, she'd have never guessed would have occurred.

Not expecting to recognize anyone else in the audience, her gaze skipped over the handsome man seated in the last row. Blinking, she looked back and smiled when she saw her friend Gray Christensen beaming at her.

Gray must have gotten back early from his seminar at Quantico. Dani was happy to see him and hoped he'd stick around after the announcement.

Since he was the lead detective on the Normalton police force, surely he'd have the most up-to-date info on the explosion victim's identity.

Now she just had to figure out a way to make him share that information.

Chapter 22

Spencer glanced at his four detainees as he drove the campus security car out of the union parking lot and headed toward his office. Charity Greathouse, leader of the Social and Economic Realities Foundation, was rocking back and forth in the front passenger seat making pitiful mewling sounds. Her perfectly manicured nails were digging into the armrest and tears were streaming down her cheeks.

Spencer felt a twinge of sympathy. Despite their age, most of the college students were far from grown up. They had learned how to act like an adult in public, but the veneer was pretty thin in a crisis situation.

Charity had been crying since Spencer had rounded up the protestors and escorted them to his vehicle. She seemed to be under the impression her parents would quit paying for her to attend the university's MBA program if they found out what she'd been doing with her spare time.

The other three activists occupying the backseat maintained absolute silence. None of them had uttered a word since Detective Taylor had handed them over to Spencer and asked him to hold them at the campus security building.

Spencer kept expecting one of them to demand a lawyer or tell him he had no right to hold them, but so far, this was as quiet as he'd ever seen this particular trio. Maybe they had finally realized that they no longer had the upper hand.

Once someone died and the police became involved, their situation had gone from a college caper to serious trouble. Spencer thought they'd have figured it out after the explosion yesterday, but it seemed that the students thought of themselves as untouchable. At least until now.

While Spencer had been hustling the quartet out of the ballroom, he'd been looking over his shoulder trying to locate Dani. He hadn't been able to spot her, and he hoped she wouldn't be too upset if he missed the announcement of the Chili Challenge winner.

He needed to text her as soon as he was able to turn the protestors over to the officer Taylor was sending for them. Fingers crossed she'd understand that he had no choice but to cooperate with the police.

Spencer ground his teeth in frustration. Finally free of his ex-wife, he'd been making progress with Dani. She'd started to trust him, and their relationship was progressing in the right direction.

She still wasn't comfortable being intimate with him, but he could wait. Whether Dani believed it yet or not, Spencer was planning a future with her.

He knew he'd been neglecting Dani this weekend, but there was never enough time. Between keeping the campus secure, guarding against any more disruption at the contest, and investigating the damage that had already occurred, he'd been working nearly twenty-four hours a day. The police may have been lead on the homicide, but the explosion had happened on his turf.

Spencer clenched his jaw as he pulled his vehicle up to the campus security building. He didn't see any patrol car parked nearby. Where was the cop Taylor had promised him?

Sighing, he told his passengers to get out, then escorted them inside. It was heading toward one o'clock, and the contest winner would be announced soon.

As he and his charges climbed the front steps, he shook his head. He hadn't tasted the recipe Dani had settled on, but he hoped she had finally figured out the magic combination and came through to win the challenge. He knew she could use the prize money.

Spencer led the foursome through the entrance and into the ground level conference room. He told them to sit down and keep quiet, then stationed himself just outside the door.

Ignoring the urge to call Dani, he hurriedly

dialed his boss. Dr. Kayley had already been informed about the protestors and was none too pleased to hear that he was helping the Normalton police take the activists into custody.

Spencer waited until she stopped yelling at him, then explained, "I only agreed because I figured it would be less of a spectacle for me to take them from the union than for the cops to storm the place and do it."

"Well," Dr. Kayley wavered, "I suppose that's true. And you say they aren't arresting the students, only taking them in for questioning?"

"As far as I know, yes."

Dr. Kayley paused, then asked, "Have you suggested to the students they should call a lawyer?"

Spencer swallowed his first answer and instead said, "It's not my, or the university's place, to protect them. They are all over twenty-one and should be held responsible for their actions."

"You don't like these students very much, do you?" Dr. Kayley's tone was icy.

Spencer frowned. It wasn't exactly that he disliked them, it was more that he thought they should have a little more world experience before trying inflict their opinions on others.

"They are welcome to protest all they want, but these kids didn't care if what they perceive as their rights interfere with the rights of others." Spencer attempted to explain his feelings to his boss. "Their belief that only their viewpoint matters is a slippery slope. And it might very well have already resulted in someone's death."

Spencer paced the length of the hallway while he waited for Dr. Kayley's response. Maybe this job wasn't for him after all.

Finally, she said, "I can see your point. But as a representative of the university, I must insist that while you should certainly cooperate with the police, you do not do their job for them."

"Gotcha."

After disconnecting, he sent Dani a hasty text. SORRY I HAD TO LEAVE. I'LL TRY TO MAKE IT BACK TO THE BALLROOM IN TIME FOR THE BIG ANNOUNCEMENT, BUT IF I DON'T, BREAK A LEG!

While he waited for the promised police officer to arrive, Spencer thought about the explosion. Taylor had said they were close to finding out who had died in the fire, and he would let Spencer know as soon as the identification had been made.

As far as Spencer had been able to determine, no one was missing from the contest. All the judges, contestants, and workers were accounted for. Certainly, if anyone from the media was missing, they would have heard about it by now, so that left an outsider.

Once they found out the who, maybe they could figure out the why, which would probably lead them to the perpetrator. Spencer could call in a few favors in order to get some information, but without any authority, his options were limited. He needed the power of a badge, or at least to keep Detective Taylor on friendly terms.

It was nearly half an hour before the promised cop arrived. She apologized and explained that she had been waiting for a second officer to show up as they could only transport two suspects in a single vehicle.

With the clock ticking, he waved away her thanks and impatiently watched her and the second cop load the protestors into the squad cars and pull away.

As soon as they were out of sight, he hopped into his truck and raced toward the union. It took him less than five minutes to park and run up the stairs to the ballroom.

He jogged toward the front and was disappointed to see that almost everyone was gone. His shoulders slumped and he turned to leave, but then he spotted Dani.

She was standing off to the side with some guy.

Spencer squinted. What was Gray Christensen doing back in town and why was he holding Dani's hand?

Spencer frowned and opened his mouth to call to them, but before he could say anything his cell phone vibrated. He read the text, then ran for the stairs.

Chapter 23

Dani ground her teeth. That had been a major letdown. It was ridiculous. She couldn't believe the words that had come out of Wallace Zorillo's mouth.

As she watched the media hurry to follow the company president out of the ballroom, her fellow contestants rush away, and the audience leave, Dani's exhaustion kept her pinned to her seat.

Jonas approached her, gave her a one-armed hug, and said, "I'll be right back and drive you home, but I really need to use the restroom first."

"Sure, Dad." Dani waved him off. "I'll meet you by the elevator."

She was staring at the ceiling when a touch on her arm startled her, and she jumped to her feet. Clutching her chest, she smiled at the handsome man in front of her. She hadn't realized that Gray had stayed behind.

"That was an anticlimax." Gray shook his head.

Dani nodded her agreement, then said, "I'm shocked that the company gave in and postponed the announcement of the winner."

"Yeah. But once that woman's husband charged in and threaten to sue if her entry was disqualified, I sort of knew they'd have to suspend the proceedings and check with their own attorneys."

"But Jill fired a gun."

"Which is against the law, but depending on the way the contest rules are written, may not be enough to disqualify her from the competition." Gray shrugged. "I'm not a lawyer, but as a detective, I've seen people get away with a lot due to loopholes."

"So do you think that means Jill would have been the winner?"

"Not necessarily." Gray leaned against the wall. "My guess is that they didn't even taste her dish. Which is why the judges and the samples were moved to another room. They're probably warming up everyone's offering and starting over."

Shoving a stray strand of hair behind her ear, Dani said, "Well at least, chili reheats well."

"I wonder how many people will be able to make the dinner tonight to hear them announce who did win?" Gray frowned. "I assume some of the contestants have to be home and at work tomorrow."

Dani pursed her mouth. "Good point. That's probably why Mr. Zorillo said attendance wasn't mandatory to win."

"Are you going?"

"I'm not sure." She tilted her head. "You heard about the explosion and the resulting fatality?"

Gray sighed. "Oh, yeah. Chief Cleary phoned and filled me in."

"Well, because of that death and the sabotage to the contest leading up to it, I promised Spencer that I wouldn't go anywhere alone." Dani bit her lip. "I'll have to see if anyone is free to come with me tonight before I decide whether I'll be there or not."

Gray frowned. "I'd offer, but the chief wants me to assist Taylor on the case, so I'll probably be working."

"Solving that homicide is much more important," Dani assured him, then asked, "Do they know who the victim is yet?"

"Not that I heard, but I'm heading to the station to meet with Taylor and hopefully there's been some developments since I talked to the chief."

Dani gestured toward the door. "You should get going then."

Gray took her hand. "I'll walk you to your van. Spencer's right that you shouldn't be alone."

"My dad's in the restroom. He'll escort me home." Dani squeezed Gray's fingers. "You can turn guard duty over to him at the elevators. I told him I'd meet him there."

* * *

Jonas pulled his Lincoln into Dani's driveway and asked, "Do you want me to pick you up for the dinner tonight?"

"I'm not sure if I'm going yet." Dani was so tired she felt like she could sleep for the next week.

Jonas fingers tightened on the steering wheel, then he said, "You really should go."

Dani raised an eyebrow. "Why is that?"

"The company went to a lot of work and expense organizing this event, and it certainly hasn't gone as well as it could have." Jonas sighed. "I just would like our family to be there to show our support."

"I can understand that." Dani opened her door and slid out.

"Besides, if you're the winner, you want to be able to collect your prize."

Dani leaned back into the car's interior. "Okay. But I can't stay very late. I'll have to be up early tomorrow to make the Lunch-to-Go meals."

"So, shall I pick you up?"

"Let me check with Spencer." Dani waved at her dad and started to shut the car door. "But if I do come with him, we can all still sit together."

Jonas shouted through the closed window, "It starts at six. Don't be late." Without waiting for a response, he tapped the horn and backed out of the driveway.

Khan met Dani as she walked through the kitchen door. His tail was wagging so hard his whole rear end was swaying. She stooped to pet him.

As Dani put down her purse and apron, she looked around and then said to the dog, "You know you aren't supposed to be in here. Where's Atti?"

He shook his head as if to say, he had no idea, then with a flick of his ears he trotted toward the cupboard where Dani kept his treats.

Dani risked the wrath of Khan by ignoring his silent demand and instead poking her head into the hallway and calling out, "Anyone home?"

When she didn't get a response, she checked the whiteboard on the wall near the door. Ivy, Tippi, and Starr were all signed out. Atti, Frannie, and Justin rarely remembered to update their whereabouts and the spaces next to their names were blank.

However, there was a message from Atti saying that she'd be back by five. She also asked that anyone seeing the note let Khan out to do his business and then give him a reward.

Sighing, Dani turned back to the kitchen. Khan was waiting and gave an impatient woof.

"Potty?" Dani asked.

Khan walked over to her and pawed at the floor, his signal to go out.

Dani snapped on his leash and opened the back door. He quickly watered a nearby bush, then when they returned to the kitchen he immediately went back to pacing by the cupboard.

After feeding Khan a few pieces of dried chicken chunks, Dani grabbed a Tupperware bowl from the freezer and headed upstairs. She shed her clothes in the bedroom, then walked into the bathroom and turned on the shower.

She texted Spencer about the dinner, then while she waited for the water to get hot—it had a long way to come from the water heater on the first floor to the third story—she opened the plastic container and grabbed one of her homemade bourbon cranberry thumbprint cookies. She devoured it and two more before stepping under the spray.

Once she had showered, blown dried her hair, and gotten dressed for the dinner, Dani checked her phone. There was no response from Spencer to her message.

She frowned. She'd read his text about missing the judging and trying to make it, but clearly, he was still tied up with campus security. It was already after five o'clock.

Guess she was going to the dinner with her father after all.

Chapter 24

Dani and Jonas arrived at the French Country House a few minutes before six, and Jonas quickly hustled Dani out of the car and into the building. He muttered about being late, as he practically dragged her down the long hallway and into the private dining room.

Dani had been surprised that Mr. Zorillo had been able to book this restaurant on such short notice. It was very popular, and reservations were tough to get. Dani wondered how the management were able to round up the extra staff to hold the contest banquet here at the last minute.

Her question was partially answered when she saw that the dinner was buffet style. That was a smart choice. The restaurant could cook whatever food they had on hand and needed only one server per twenty to thirty guests.

Dani and her dad located their table, then headed to the bar at the rear of the room. Jonas ordered a vodka martini, but Dani stuck to Diet Coke. She was too tired to risk consuming alcohol and losing control of her tongue.

When Jonas stepped away to greet Wallace

Zorillo, the bartender said, "I hear you all had quite a bit of excitement at the cooking contest."

"Oh?" Dani tried to keep her voice neutral.

Since they'd had a lot of problems at the Chili Challenge, and what had happened during the event wasn't exactly a secret, the guy wasn't completely out of line. Still, she was unsure why the man chose to strike up a conversation with her.

"You don't remember me, do you?" The guy chuckled. "My name's Boogie. I was the bartender at the engagement party where the tent blew over. Remember, I was the one who told you that bartenders were really pharmacists with limited inventory?"

Dani chuckled. "Yep, that was a good one."

"Trouble seems to follow you, doesn't it?" Boogie waggled his eyebrows.

Taking a long drink of her soda, Dani sighed. "It sure seems to." Then she brightened. "So, have you heard much about the incidents?"

"The usual." Boogie pushed a dish of snack mix toward Dani, who helped herself to a peanut. "Rumor has it that they identified the victim, but they aren't releasing the name yet."

"Really?" Dani's thoughts immediately flew to Spencer. Maybe that was why he wasn't returning her texts. If they knew who had been killed, he'd probably been called down to the police department. "Guess they have to notify the next of kin first."

"Yeah."

Dani narrowed her eyes. "So, who told you they know who the deceased's identity?"

"Let's just say one of the chicks that I'm dating is a clerk in the ME's office." Boogie winked.

"But she didn't tell you the name?" Being a big fan of monogamy, Dani was a little put off when he'd said *one* of the girls he was seeing.

She examined him. He was only an inch or so taller than she was, with green eyes and red hair. She didn't know his age, but guessed he was in his early twenties. He didn't fit her picture of a ladies' man, but then again, her taste didn't always mesh with the majority's preferences.

Boogie shook his head. "Nah, she knows I have a big mouth and didn't want to get fired."

"Hmm." Dani took a sip of her drink. "Anything else about the contest?"

Boogie sliced a lime. "Well, I heard the gal who shot off her gun is out on bail."

"I suppose that means she's here."

Sadly, Dani wasn't surprised. If her husband could get the contest to allow her entry, he sure as heck could get her out of jail.

"Right there." Boogie pointed over Dani's

shoulder.

She turned around and spotted Jill and her spouse chatting with Scottie Diller. No doubt, making sure the radio personality heard their side of the gun incident story.

Boogie and Dani chatted for a few minutes more, then Dani walked over to join her father, who was in deep discussion with Wallace Zorillo.

Just as she arrived at her dad's side, a voice over the P.A. system announced, "Dinner is served."

Jonas hustled Dani over to the buffet, barely making it there before a line formed behind them. She made her selections, then followed her dad to their table.

As she sat down, she spotted an arm waving. Not surprisingly, it was Frannie. She waved back and the woman made her way over to Dani and took the chair next to her.

Although she was fond of Frannie, she had been trying to avoid the eager journalist. Unwilling to have her words quoted in *The Normalton News*, Dani had been ducking the rookie reporter since the explosion.

While Frannie was greeting everyone, her fiancé, Justin Howard, arrived and plopped down in the last available seat, which happened to be next to Jonas. Dani's father had met the journalist duo and shared Spencer's feeling about them. Neither man appreciated being under the media's microscope.

Before Dani could figure out a graceful getaway, Frannie demanded, "Where have you been? I've been looking for you all weekend."

"Around." Dani gave up on her escape plans and spread her napkin on her lap. "You know, cooking." No matter what she did, this conversation was happening.

Frannie narrowed her eyes. "Every time I saw you, you disappeared before I could get over to you."

"It's been a busy weekend." Dani picked up her fork and poked at the food on her plate.

She'd been excited to eat at the French Country House, hoping to be able to order their signature Beef Wellington. Instead, the choice of main courses at the buffet had consisted of sliced roast, fried chicken, and mostaccioli. The same old menu featured at so many catered events.

"Dani had to concentrate on her chili." Dani's father spoke between bites. "She couldn't allow herself to be distracted by the press."

Before Frannie could respond, Elvis, who was seated between Mick Owen and Tory Mays, said, "How about we all answer your question now, little lady. We ain't got nothin' to hide. Right, folks?"

"Can't we just eat in peace?" Jonas glared at Elvis, then turned his laser stare on Frannie.

Leaning around his wife, Eric asked, "Was everyone pleased with how their contest entry turned out?"

"I was pretty happy," Dani answered, grateful for the man's attempt to change the subject.

Elvis puffed out his chest. "Mine was great."

"Well, even though I had to spend some of my precious cooking time guarding against that awful Jill VanAsden, my chili is definitely a winner," Tory boasted.

Frannie leaned forward and asked, "What happened with Jill?"

"I know she was the one behind all the sabotage. I heard her bragging on her cell that she had the prize in the bag." Tory shook her head. "I can't believe they let her back into the contest after almost killing us all with that gun of hers."

Frannie's brown eyes sparkled in anticipation. "Do you have any evidence Jill was causing the other problems?"

"Uh." Tory glanced at her husband and Eric nodded. "We had a nanny cam set up in my area and caught her switching my homegrown chili powder for a generic brand."

Justin frowned. "Then why didn't you turn her in to the authorities?"

With everyone staring at her, Tory's mouth

opened and closed, but no words came out. She turned to her husband who whispered frantically in her ear.

"I think I know." Dani played the last few days over in her mind, then gestured toward the now silent couple. "They were keeping that little piece of information up their sleeves as a last resort. If Jill won, they would have produced the recording, but in the meantime, if she messed up some of the other contestants' recipes, all the better for Tory's chance of winning."

Frannie tapped furiously on the tablet she'd produced from her tote bag. "Is that true?"

"We were under no obligation to help police the contest." Eric crossed his arms. "And if UFE couldn't protect the competitors, that was on them not us."

Dani flinched. She was amazed at how cutthroat the challenge had become. She'd had a totally different picture of how things would go.

Before Dani could continue her fretting, Justin asked, "I wonder if that means that Jill was the one who interfered with the propane tank that exploded."

"I don't think so, but I suppose it depends on when the tank was messed with." Elvis tilted his head. "Because I saw Jill and her husband at the local pancake joint fifteen or twenty minutes before the explosion."

Shoot! Dani's heart skipped a beat. She'd hope they had their culprit. Still, she'd better text Gray with what she'd learned. He could decide if it was worth investigating or not.

Dani brooded while everyone else finished their meal. What was it about Jill's alibi that bothered her?

Chapter 25

"And then, Tory Mays tells us that she and her husband had a nanny cam in her workspace and caught Jill VanAsden messing with her ingredients." Dani shook her head.

Spencer had been waiting on the mansion's front porch when Jonas dropped off Dani at home. After grabbing drinks from the kitchen, they had settled in the family room.

Dani had mostly furnished this room by shopping at the secondhand stores, but she and Spencer were sharing the cocoa nailhead-on-velvet sofa that she had discovered on the curb of Normalton's ritziest suburb.

It had been put out for the trash collector, but the owner had been happy to let her haul it away. The small wine stain on the back was easily covered by a throw blanket and she'd seen that same couch for sale for well over three thousand dollars.

Dani got comfortable with her back to the armrest and continued, "Can you believe the Mays kept the identity of the saboteur a secret? How can they live with themselves after making everyone run around wasting their time trying to figure it out?"

Spencer took her foot and began to knead her heel. "People like that have no empathy. No sense of community."

"Yeah. I'm just glad she didn't win the contest." Dani closed her eyes and enjoyed the sensation that Spencer's fingers were producing. After having been on her feet for so many hours the past few days, his massage was heavenly.

"How do you feel about coming in second?" He moved onto Dani's arch, and she sighed in pleasure. "If Elvis hadn't come back, you would have won first place."

"True. But he did and there's nothing I can do about it." Dani opened her eyelids a crack. "Will the Mays get in trouble for withholding evidence?"

"At the time, it wasn't a police investigation and after the explosion they could always claim it slipped their mind, so the only way they could be held accountable would be if UFE or the university sued them."

"Well, that sucks," Dani said half to herself, then asked, "How about Jill?"

"She'll get her hand slapped for firing a gun, but again, the sabotage is a civil matter." Spencer switched feet and started rubbing her left one. "Unless, of course, she was the one who vandalized the propane tank, which resulted in the explosion and death."

"Speaking of which, I heard that the victim had been identified." Dani narrowed her eyes. "Do you know who it was? Is that why you were radio silent for so long?"

"Yes and yes." Spencer finished with her feet and moved on to her calves.

"And...?"

Spencer sighed, "It was my absent security guard, Warren Douglas. The medal they found had his name engraved on the back and once the ME was pointed in the right direction they obtained dental records, which matched the body."

"Wait! How is that possible? Didn't he quit?"

"Evidently, he didn't really resign. Someone else must have left that message that was supposedly from him."

"Hmm." Dani paused. "Does that mean his death wasn't an accident?"

Spencer nodded. "That's the new theory. But now the question is, was Douglas the target or did the killer see they'd gotten the wrong person and leave the message to cover up until they could do away with whoever they were really aiming for?"

They were both quiet for a while and Dani was dozing off when Spencer asked, "Do you know any reason that VanAsden woman would want Douglas dead?"

"No. How would she even know him?" A thought nibbled on the edge of Dani's consciousness. What was it? She concentrated. No. It was gone, but another idea popped into her head. "Anyway, Elvis said he saw Jill and her husband at a local pancake place having breakfast the morning of the explosion, so she even if she was the one who vandalized the propane tank, she wouldn't have any idea who the victim was. Whoever called in Douglas's resignation had to be around to see the guard go up in flames."

"Good point." Spencer pulled out a notepad from his shirt pocket. "I need to make a note to talk to Elvis."

Dani teased, "You mean give Gray a heads-up to interview Elvis."

"Right." Spencer frowned. "By the way, I saw him with you in the union ballroom, when did he get back into town?"

Noting Spencer's unhappy expression, Dani wondered what that was about, then mentally shrugged and said, "Right before the announcement that they weren't naming the winner until tonight. The police chief called Gray and ordered him to return to town immediately and assist Detective Taylor."

"Oh."

"Anyway, I've told you everything I learned today. What about you?"

"Taylor asked me to corral the students who had caused the ruckus during the contest, which I did, and then I had to wait for their official escort to arrive for them." Spencer's brow wrinkled. "Other than that, I spent most of my time cooling my heels at the police station. They called me in when Douglas was identified as the victim, but as usual everything connected with this case is hurry up and wait."

"Did you hear anything about the interviews they did with the protestors?"

"Not yet."

Dani tsked, then said, "You should ask Gray when you call him about Elvis."

"I will, but I'll probably have better luck with the chief." Spencer rolled his shoulders. "I've requested an appointment."

Dani noticed how tired Spencer looked. "Will she meet with you?"

"Yeah." Spencer leaned forward and picked up his bottle of water. "She's pretty cooperative."

"Now that everyone has left town, won't it make the investigation even more difficult?" Dani took a sip of her Diet Coke.

Spencer grimaced. "If they left. I'm guessing the police will have asked everyone to stick around for a few days. And if they're all gone, the cops will start with the locals."

"Great." Dani groaned. "That means me."

"Yeah, but you have an airtight alibi." Spencer's grin was devilish. "But there are two local judges and some of the media."

"The media is under suspicion?"

"To a certain degree. But mostly the police will just want to know what they saw during the events.

Dani nodded thoughtfully. "None of the journalists will give that info up easily."

"No." Spencer tipped his head. "Which is why you and I should see what we can get out of Frannie and Justin."

"They won't tell us either."

"Not if we ask directly. But if we're just shooting the breeze over dinner…" Spencer raised a brow.

"Are you suggesting a double date?"

"Yes."

"When?" Dani tilted her head, thinking. "I'm free tomorrow night, but then I'm jammed the rest of the week."

"Perfect. Ask Frannie in the morning, then let me know if it's a go."

"Why are we doing this?" Dani narrowed her eyes. "You're usually the one telling me to let the police handle things."

"Because someone killed one of *my* men on *my* campus." Spencer's voice was flat. "It's my responsibility to get justice for both."

Chapter 26

Dani got up and Spencer followed her into the kitchen. "If Warren Douglas was the intended victim, do you have a suspect?"

"No. I don't really know much about him." Spencer leaned a hip against the counter. "I'll need to review his employment file and see if that gives me any leads."

"We should look at his social media accounts." Dani rinsed out her glass and put it on the drainer. "Do you have someone on staff that's good at that sort of thing?"

Spencer stepped behind her, slipping his arms around her waist. "Unfortunately, the guy I had covering online stuff quit a few weeks ago. He got a better offer from a private company."

"Well." Dani found it hard to think with his warm breath fanning the sensitive spot below her ear. "Maybe Ivy can help us out. She's a whiz at hunting down accounts and connections."

Spencer's nuzzling was interrupted by a yawn. "Sorry," he murmured, then added, "I don't want to involve Ivy. I'll get one of my other guys to give it a try. We need someone to step into that role anyway."

"I'll bet you're exhausted. How much rest have you had since the whole Chili Challenge started?" Dani turned to face him, tracing a fingertip across his lip. "You should go home and get some sleep."

Slowly and seductively his gaze slid downward. "I think I'm getting my second wind."

Her heart jolted and her pulse pounded. His appeal was undeniable. His hands burrowed under hair and caressed the nape of her neck. Dani inhaled sharply at the contact, a shiver rippling through her.

He whispered into her neck, "You're driving me crazy. I can't concentrate. I think about you all the time."

She stared into his blue eyes. She'd been putting off taking the next step with Spencer. It wasn't that she didn't want to or that she didn't trust him, it was more that she didn't trust herself.

It had taken them a while to get to this point and somewhere in the back of her mind, she was still afraid that what they had wouldn't last. She'd never had good luck with men, and even her father's unexpected change of heart didn't reassure her.

In fact, for some reason, the more Jonas became a part of her life and acted like the dad she'd always dreamed of having, the more her fears regarding Spencer increased. She wanted to tell him how much he meant to her, but the words refused to push past her lips.

As Dani's thoughts raced, Spencer steady gaze never left her face. The longer she was silent, the harder he stared.

After a while his broad shoulders drooped and he said, "You're right. I probably should go home and get some sleep."

The hurt in his eyes tore her apart and instead of letting him go, she gathered him close and pressed her lips to his, trying to show him how she felt with her kiss.

His lips devoured hers, and the room spun.

* * *

Dani fumbled for her phone, the blaring alarm boring into her skull like it was trying to perform a lobotomy. It felt as if she had just fallen asleep, but the red numbers assured her that it was five-thirty.

She needed to get up and get cracking on the Lunch-to-Go bags or they'd never be done by the time her customers arrived.

As she threw on a pair of yoga pants and a T-shirt, then scraped her hair into a ponytail, emotions from the night before kept flickering through her mind. The disappointment at not winning first prize coupled with the warm feeling of her dad being supportive about her loss and telling her second place was great. Then the end of the evening with Spencer.

She was truly a lucky woman to have such an understanding man in her life. He'd accepted that all she was offering was a few passionate kisses and left her with a sweet smile.

Dani was still marveling at her good fortune when she made it into the kitchen and checked the whiteboard for today's sous-chef. Seeing that it was Atti's turn to assist, Dani was a little surprised that the girl hadn't arrived yet.

Atti was usually on time, if not early. She was extremely grateful to have a roof over her head and a steady supply of food. Unlike Dani's other boarders who had never known a day of hunger or a night with nowhere to sleep, Atti was intent on hanging on to what she knew was a good thing.

Tippi, Ivy, and Starr had already finished breakfast and gone upstairs to get ready for their classes when Atti flew through the back door and headed straight for the coffee pot.

She muttered an apology for being late and took a gulp from her cup. Dani was alarmed at how drained Atti looked. Was something wrong?

Her hair was unwashed and stuffed under a baseball cap, her eyelids drooped, and her whole body drooped. She ignored the bowl of oatmeal Dani slid in front of her and wrapped her hands around her mug as if she were cold.

"Everything okay?"

Atti tried to smile, but failed and said, "Yeah. It's just that Friday, one of my teachers called me in and said I had to redo a project, or he'd fail me. At first, he said I could have a week, but then he texted me the next day and said I had to bring it to his office tonight at eight."

"If you need the time, I could probably spare you this morning." Dani bit her lip, wondering how she would be able to prepare everything herself.

Atti shook her head. "Thanks. But it's cool. That's why I wasn't around the contest. I've been working on the darn thing night and day, and I'm nearly finished. I can use the break."

"Terrific!"

Dani glanced at the clock. It was a little after 7 a.m. and it would take them a couple of hours to get the food ready. Then another hour to get it packed.

Soon the scent of chocolate and caramel drifted through the air. Dani inhaled the tantalizing aroma as she prepared her delectable Cookie Dough Billionaire Bars for the Indulgent lunch bags.

Atti was quiet while she wrapped chicken breasts in bacon for the Are You My Mummy sandwich. They would also go into the Indulgent bag.

Several minutes when by before Atti finally broke the silence and asked, "Do you think it's funny that a teacher would have you come to his office so late?" Without waiting for Dani to respond, Atti continued in a shaky voice, "He said I had to bring it in person, but this guy sets off my freakometer."

Dani paused. Her first inclination was to brush off Atti's concern. The girl had major trust issues.

"Well," Dani finished mixing the shortbread crust, pressed it into the prepared sheet pan, and slid it into the preheated oven, "is there anything specific that he does that makes you uncomfortable?"

"Um." Atti wrinkled her brow as she lined up slices of peaches and prosciutto for the Healthy option's Just Peachy sandwich. "He texts me a lot."

"About class stuff?" While the shortbread baked, Dani turned her attention to the potato salad that would accompany both meals. There were two versions. The healthy one was made with Greek yogurt and olive oil, the other one used the more traditional mayo.

Before she started to spread avocado on the whole grain bread, Atti poured herself another cup of coffee. "Not always. Sometimes it's just a funny meme or some emoji."

Dani frowned, then she asked, "Can I see those texts?"

"Sure. I'll show you as soon as we finish up here."

Dani considered what Atti had told her, then asked, "Is there anything else he does that seems off?"

Atti had finished assembling both types of sandwiches and wrapping them and was silent until she was on her way to store them in the commercial-size cooler in the back of the kitchen.

Atti's voice trembled. "He always stands too close, and I've smelled alcohol on his breath."

The timer beeped and Dani fetched the shortbread crust from the oven, then put it on a rack to cool as she carefully chose her words. "I think we need to ask Spencer or Gray to look at that teacher's texts before you go to his office tonight."

Atti didn't respond right away, but after she deposited the sandwiches in the cooler she said, "Would you be able to go with me tonight?"

Dani remembered her promise to Spencer about arranging a double date with Frannie and Justin so she said, "I may not be able to, but we'll find someone who can."

Solving Warren Douglas's murder was important, but so was saving Atti from an inappropriate teacher. Dani smiled. She knew just who to ask to accompany the girl.

Chapter 27

"I'll be back at five tonight and someone will be here to go with me to see my teacher, right?" Atti stood by the backdoor biting her lip.

Dani nodded. "Definitely. I promise you there's no way I'd let you go on your own."

"Okay, then." Atti nodded. "Good. See you then."

Dani gazed after the departing teenager. Having Ivy, Tippi, and Starr living with her in the mansion and Atti and Frannie and Justin in the carriage house apartments, had turned out be as much of a blessing as inheriting Mrs. Cook's property. They were all good kids, and their rent was a big help, as were the hours the college girls worked for her as partial payment for their room and board.

Running her hand affectionately across the four-sided stainless island that held two commercial stoves, a griddle, a broiler, a salamander, a sink, a pot-filler, and a built-in ice container integrated in the countertop, Dani smiled contentedly. It was amazing that the kitchen designed by Mrs. Cook was exactly what Dani needed for her company.

She glanced at the restaurant-sized refrigerator

against the back wall. It was as if Mrs. Cook had furnished the place with Dani's dreams in mind.

Handling the trio of businesses was tough, but the mansion's setup made it a lot less stressful. The kitchen was spacious enough to prep all the food she would need for her catering gigs, and with the installation of the pass-through window that she'd had put in near the back door, it made selling the takeaway meals a snap.

Speaking of which, she had about half an hour until her lunch patrons would begin to arrive, and she needed to send a few texts. She hurried upstairs to grab her cell phone.

Thirty minutes later she walked back in the kitchen just as the service bell chimed. She straightened her apron and pasted on her professional smile, then went to greet her first customer of the day.

Sliding open the window, Dani recognized one of her regulars, Kenna, a freshman from a small town about an hour north of Normalton, and said, "Good morning, which lunch do you want today?"

"My day already sucks, so I'll take the Indulgent." The girl tapped her credit card on the machine attached to the narrow shelf.

As Dani handed over the red-and-white-striped paper bag, she asked, "What happened?"

"I ran into someone I thought I'd never have to see again."

Raising a brow, Dani said, "An old boyfriend?"

"Worse. A mean girl from my high school." Kenna grimaced. "She was supposed to be going to a fancy college in the east. But there she was, walking down the hall of my dorm with a bunch of my friends following her like baby ducks."

Dani wrinkled her nose. "I take it her personality hadn't improved?"

"Nope." Kenna made a face. "If anything, she was even nastier. I asked her what she was doing at NU, and she ignored me, winked at my so-called friends, and said, 'Remember, you agreed to ignore her.' Then they just all walked away."

Dani patted Kenna's hand. "I'm so sorry. Maybe, in a few days, they'll see through her."

"Or maybe I'll add some poison to her perfume and put us all out of our misery." Kenna giggled.

Dani shook her head and warned, "Don't even joke about that."

"Right. Not in today's supersensitive atmosphere. Anyway," Kenna waved, "see you tomorrow."

Grimacing, Dani watched the girl hop onto her bike and head toward the university. She hoped Kenna's nemesis wouldn't cause her too much anguish. It was sad that someone's fresh start could be ruined by a ghost from their past.

Dani turned away from the window and started toward the coffee pot, her mind racing. Warren Douglas had told Spencer he wanted a new beginning, could a phantom from his previous life be the one who killed him?

That is, of course, if he were even the intended victim. Shrugging, Dani poured a cup of coffee and got back to work.

It was a little after two by the time Dani sold the last Lunch-to-Go and finished cleaning up the kitchen. Searching for her cell, she remembered that she'd left it in her suite, and ran upstairs to get it.

She noticed two missed messages. One was the person she'd asked to escort Atti to her teacher's office that evening saying he'd be happy to help. The other was from Frannie indicating that she and Justin would love to have dinner with Dani and Spencer.

Dani let Spencer know that their double date was on, then decided to take a nap. She was still exhausted from the Chili Challenge weekend and getting Frannie and Justin to talk tonight would be a challenge.

A couple of hours later, Dani woke to the chime of the front doorbell. She closed her eyes. Maybe if she ignored them, whoever it was would go away, but the ringing persisted.

Finally, she got up and went downstairs. She was in no hurry, still hoping the person would leave. If it was a prospective client, they needed to call and make an appointment.

When Dani arrived at the door, she looked through the peephole and saw a man dressed in a blue polo shirt with an emblem she didn't recognize embroidered on the pocket. He was bald and his eyes were hidden behind mirrored sunglasses.

Who in the world was on her front porch? She considered ignoring him, but as she turned away, he must have sensed her presence and the frequency of the ringing increased.

Fine. She'd open the door, but she was definitely keeping the chain on. "May I help you?"

"Victor Josephson at your service, ma'am." He thrust his hand through the small gap. "And you must be Dani Sloan."

"I am." She ignored his hand, and he slowly withdrew it. "What is it you want?"

"I'd like to have a word with you, if you have a moment." His request sounded more like an order.

Dani bristled. "About what?"

"It's a little complicated. Perhaps we could sit down inside?"

Dani shook her head. "I'm sorry, Mr. Josephson,

I don't have time right now. Perhaps we could schedule something tomorrow."

"If you could just give me fifteen minutes," he persisted. "I need to talk to you about the Chili Challenge."

"What about it?" After a few minutes of silence, she prodded, "I'm not letting a stranger inside my home, so either talk or leave."

The man took off his sunglasses and placed them in his shirt pocket. "I'm the CEO of USA Foodservice Equipment, and the contest was supposed to be good publicity for our company. To take the public's mind off our China associations."

"Yeah. I heard that had become a problem for your company."

Josephson cleared his throat. "I understand you and the chief of campus security are seeing each other."

"So? Our relationship's not exactly a secret."

"I wonder if you'd be willing to pass on any information Mr. Drake may share with you?"

Dani tilted her head. "Why would I do that?"

"Because my company would pay you a hefty consultant fee and throw any local catering business your way."

Dani pursed her lips, then asked, "Why do you need a spy?"

Josephson gave her an appraising look. "Let's just say that my company needs to get ahead of anything negative that may be revealed as a result of the investigation."

"And the police aren't cooperating." Dani didn't trust this man. Not one little bit.

"We have ears on the force, but from what my people tell me, Mr. Drake will be conducting his own investigation."

Dani kept her expression impassive. "Possibly. But what makes you think he'll tell me anything?"

"My dear, don't be so modest." Josephson ran his fingers over his head. "From what I hear, Mr. Drake is infatuated with you, and the two of you have solved crimes together before."

"Interesting." Dani forced herself not to beam. It felt wonderful to hear that people thought Spencer was in love with her. "But even if that is true, or maybe because that might be true, I'm not willing to reveal anything Spencer might confide in me."

"Before you decide," Josephson stared into her eyes. "How would you feel if you were the reason your father lost his job?"

His question caught her unprepared. If he had asked it a few months ago she might have said she didn't care. But now, that she and Jonas were forging a better relationship, she couldn't just throw him to the wolves.

Could she?

Chapter 28

After reluctantly accepting the CEO's business card, Dani closed the door and leaned against the smooth wood. Her emotions were at war. There had to be a solution that didn't involve getting her father fired or betraying Spencer, didn't there?

After several minutes, she sighed and started up the stairs to get ready for her double date. She had until one o'clock tomorrow afternoon to figure out what to do. And she would need every minute.

But first she had to introduce Atti to her bodyguard. Dani smiled for the first time since Josephson had shown up. Atti's sleezy teacher had no idea about the can of whoop-ass she was about to unleash on him.

Once Dani was finished dressing, she went downstairs and waited on the front porch for her guest. He was exactly on time, and she gave him a quick hug, then invited him to sit down until Atti arrived.

Dani had met Udell Williams when she catered an engagement party for his boss, the owner of the local baseball team. He was an enormous young man, certainly big enough to make an unscrupulous professor think twice before he ever sexually harassed one of his students again.

Dani had looked over the texts that the man had sent Atti, then consulted with Spencer. They both agreed that the community college instructor was up to no good.

Udell took a seat and gave Dani a sweet smile. "Moms says thank you for sending all those cakes and cookies for her church's bake sale. They made enough to put a new roof on the building."

"She is very welcome." Dani felt her cheeks redden. She'd told Mrs. Williams to keep her contribution anonymous. "It's a relief that the congregation won't have to worry about any more interior damage."

"Yeah. I'm going home in a couple of days to help with the construction." He ducked his head. "I'm just glad I was still here when you texted. Fill me in on what this douchebag is doing to your friend."

Dani explained what Atti had told her and summarized the texts, then added, "She's only nineteen, but she was homeless for a while. Although she's probably handled a lot worse situations than this jerk, for some reason, she seemed really shook up about facing him alone."

"It's harder to stand up to someone who holds your future in their hands than to a creep just trying to get over on you." Udell slid a glance at Dani, who nodded her understanding.

"Hey! Where is everyone?" Atti's voice interrupted her thoughts, but Dani tucked away what Udell had said to think about later.

"On the porch!" she shouted, then watched as Atti burst through the front door juggling several bags and boxes.

Dani made the introductions, smiling to herself when she noticed the spark of interest flicker between Atti and Udell. They all chatted for a few minutes, then Udell took the cartons from Atti's arms and escorted her to his car.

Once everything was safely in the trunk of the old Buick, and Atti was settled in the passenger seat, Udell slid in behind the wheel. He beeped the horn at Dani, waved, and carefully reversed onto the road.

A few seconds later, Spencer pulled into the driveway. They were meeting Frannie and Justin at the restaurant, so Dani didn't wait for him to get out of his truck. Instead, she ran down the steps. Then once he stopped the pickup, she opened the passenger door and climbed inside.

Spencer greeted her, and after a quick kiss, asked, "Where we going?"

"Uno, Dos, Tequila."

"Is that the new Mexican restaurant by NU?"

Spencer asked. When Dani nodded, he continued, "I thought you weren't too fond of Mexican food."

Dani shrugged. "It's not my favorite, but Frannie wanted to try it, so I thought it was a good idea to go with her choice and keep her happy."

"You're probably right." Spencer headed toward campus town, then asked, "How was your day?"

Dani flipped down the visor, dug a tube of lip gloss out of her purse, and said, "Busy, with a lot of surprises." She told him how she solved Atti's problem.

"Good idea. Udell will settle that guy's hash."

Dani nodded, then asked, "How was your day?"

"I met with the police chief in the morning and in the afternoon with my boss." Spencer gripped the steering wheel tightly. "She isn't at all happy with the way the Chili Challenge weekend turned out."

Dani frowned. "And she blames you?"

"Not exactly, but she would like everyone to forget about the sabotages and murder."

Dani snorted, "Wouldn't we all?"

Chuckling, Spencer pulled into the restaurant's minuscule parking lot. It was packed, but someone was leaving. He applied the brakes and put on his turn signal.

As they waited, Dani asked, "So, did the police chief share any news about either of those issues?"

"Actually, yes. You'll never guess..." Spencer stopped and concentrated on inserting his huge pickup into the tight space.   Just as he managed to squeeze it between the narrow lines and open his door, Frannie and Justin appeared.

As Spencer helped Dani from the truck, he whispered, "I'll tell you later."

Dani gritted her teeth; she hated when people did that, but she pasted a smile on her face and nodded. Once they had greeted the other couple, they entered the restaurant.

They were immediately escorted to one of the few empty tables, and Dani raised her eyebrows.

Frannie giggled. "Power of the press. I called ahead and told them that I was writing a review for the paper."

"And are you?" Dani tilted her head.

"I am now."

Spencer ordered a Dos Equis, the women wanted frozen margaritas, and Justin went with a Dr Pepper. Their drinks were delivered along with a basket of warm tortilla chips and bowls of salsa and guacamole.

After selecting the rest of their meal, Dani glanced at Spencer. When he gave her a slight nod, she said, "So, I bet you guys didn't think you'd get such exciting stories out of a chili contest."

"Nope." Frannie smirked. "None of the other reporters wanted to cover the event, which is how we got stuck with it. Now they're sorry."

Justin grinned. "I was able to get it on the website almost as fast as it was happening."

"You probably were watching closer and saw more than anyone else," Spencer encouraged.

"Definitely." Frannie bounced in her chair. "We split up and were able to cover almost everything. I was right there when that crazy chick fired her gun."

Dani took a sip of her drink, then asked, "How about in the beginning? When all the sabotage stuff was going on?"

"Unfortunately," Frannie sighed, "we didn't get anything the first day."

"But we weren't caught with our pants down the next one." Justin reached for the last chip, then looked at everyone. When they gestured for him to go ahead, he grabbed it and scooped up the remaining salsa. After swallowing he said, "We got there early and were the only press around when the propane tank exploded."

Dani and Spencer exchanged glances, then Dani asked, "Did you see anything suspicious?"

"Not that day," Justin answered.

Frannie slapped his arm and said, "We can't reveal anything more until our piece runs in the special section the paper is putting together about the contest and the murder."

Before Dani could continue to probe, their food arrived. As they were served, she mentally ran through ways of making Frannie talk.

They'd all ordered combo platters and as they enjoyed the different foods, Dani steered the conversation to everyday subjects like her next catering job and improvements she wanted to make in the mansion.

Spencer played along and talked about the campus security's new plan for enhancing security around the dorms. Justin and Frannie relaxed, telling stories about how difficult it was to plan a wedding back home when they weren't living there.

After they'd finished their meal and ordered dessert, Spencer turned to Frannie and said, "What if I could give you an exclusive on who was behind the original Chili Challenge sabotages? Would you tell me what you know in exchange?"

Dani's gaze darted toward Spencer, and she scowled. Had they been able to prove Jill messed with everyone's stuff, not just Tory's?

"Was it the killer?" Frannie asked excitedly.

Spencer shook his head. "No info until we have a deal."

"Hmm." Frannie leaned over to Justin, and they

held a whispered conversation. Finally, she said, "We'll tell you what we have, but you have to wait until our article hits the paper before sharing anything we say with the police."

Spencer's eyebrows disappeared into his hairline, but his voice was deceptively mild when he asked, "I take it you didn't see the person who messed with the propane tank?"

"No. But the day before we did hear two people shouting. It sounded like the guard who was killed was yelling at someone he hadn't expected to see."

Dani wrinkled her brow. An idea tickled at the back of her brain. Someone else had said something similar, and at the time she'd had a fleeting thought about the murder. What was it?

Spencer's irritated voice broke into Dani's thoughts. "Why in the hell wouldn't you tell the police that? That could be important information that they could use to solve the crime."

"Could is the operant word." Justin scoured the tabletop and found a tortilla chip that had previously escaped his notice. Popping it into his mouth, he mumbled, "As we said, the argument we heard happened the day *before* the explosion.

"And we didn't see who the guard was yelling at," Frannie hurriedly added.

"Still." A muscle ticked in Spencer's jaw. "What

you heard might be helpful."

"Which is why we'll tell you." Frannie looked between Dani and Spencer. "You two are more likely to figure out who was behind the explosion than the police."

"Maybe," Spencer admitted. "So, we have a deal?"

Frannie and Justin nodded, then Frannie said, "But you have to go first."

"Fine." Spencer waited as the server placed their desserts in front of them. Once she left, he said, "The police found evidence as to who was behind the sabotages. But during the time period when the propane tank could have been tampered with, that person was not on campus."

Frannie leaned forward. "Who was it?"

"The head of the Animal Rights group, Hamilton Butcher," Spencer announced.

"How about Tory's hidden camera catching Jill switching her chili powder?" Dani blurted out, then wished she hadn't.

Justin brayed. "Whoa! There were two saboteurs?"

"Jill provided an alibi to the police for the other incidents." Spencer took a bite of his caramel flan, then continued, "At that point, Detective Taylor turned his attention to the protestors. The rest of them could account for their time, but Butcher couldn't. They got a warrant and found a bunch of the missing stuff in his dorm room."

Frannie ate a spoonful of her fried ice cream, then asked, "If he could prove he was somewhere else when the propane tank was tinkered with, where was he? Whoever said they saw him at that time could be lying."

"Nope." Spencer snickered. "Butcher was in a holding cell in the county jail from Friday afternoon until ten a.m. Saturday. He and his cohorts attempted to free a farmer's cattle but got cornered by a bull. The farmer pressed charges for trespassing and Butcher was waiting for a bail hearing."

Dani shook her head. That was certainly an unbreakable alibi.

Spencer turned to Frannie. "Your turn."

"Friday afternoon, after everyone left the contest area and we headed to our car, I realized that I couldn't find my cell phone." Frannie paused and looked at Justin.

He took over. "We figured it had to have fallen out of her pocket somewhere between the union and the parking lot, so we retraced our route. When we got to the patio steps, we saw the security guard arguing with someone who was just out of sight."

"We tried to get closer," Frannie said. "But there

was nowhere to hide, and we settled for listening to what they were saying."

Spencer gritted his teeth and ground out, "Which was?"

"The person was yelling at the guard about hoping he'd never see him again," Frannie explained. "Then the guard said something about making it worthwhile for him to keep his mouth shut or he'd let everyone know what the other guy really was."

Dani asked, "So, the concealed person was a man?"

"The voice was definitely deep," Justin said. "I couldn't swear it was a guy, but that would be my best guess."

Spencer frowned. "And Douglas never called the guy by name?"

"No. He might have said, 'Boobie, you get that money to me before the contest starts tomorrow morning,' but the guard was nearly whispering by then."

Spencer asked, "Boobie, not Bobbie?"

"Maybe." Frannie shrugged. "We just can't be sure."

Justin added, "I checked. There are no Roberts or any variation of the name Bobbie involved in the challenge as a contestant, judge, or staff member."

"Great." Dani sighed. "Another dead end."

Chapter 29

Dani and Spencer were lingering over the last bites of their desserts when the restaurant door opened and Tippi strolled in with her boyfriend, Caleb Boyd. After a rocky start, she and the prelaw student had been dating for a few months and seemed to be settling into a steady relationship.

When Tippi spotted them, she led Caleb to their table and said, "Fancy seeing you all here. Looks like we're not the only one hankering for some chips and guac tonight."

"Who can resist all that avocado goodness?" Dani smiled and added, "You just missed Frannie and Justin."

"Darn." Tippi snapped her fingers. "Caleb has been wanting to ask Frannie about that cop she knows in Scumble River. He thinks they might be related."

Glancing at Caleb, Dani saw his cheeks turn red. The young Texan definitely didn't like being the center of attention.

"Hey, you never told me the name of that guy who died in the propane explosion." Tippi pointed at Dani. "I had to hear it around campus."

Dani snapped her fingers. "Sorry! I only found out last night and it slipped my mind that you wanted to know."

"Oh, well, no harm, no foul. I'll still be able to use it in my speech."

Before they could continue the conversation, a table opened up. Tippi and Caleb quickly ran over to claim it, then waved their goodbyes to Spencer and Dani.

Spencer picked up his spoon but before he could scoop the last bite of flan into his mouth, his cell pinged with an incoming text.

He glanced at his phone and frowned, then said, "Robert's had some luck with the new app we've been using that allows us to search most social media using hashtags and keywords." Spencer grinned. "The one I told you about that was developed by an NU student. Thank goodness she's dating one of my staff, so we've had first dibs at trying it out."

"I remember." Dani pushed her plate away and wiped her mouth with a napkin. "I hope you're paying her a fair amount for the use."

Ignoring Dani's comment, Spencer said, "Anyway, Robert found some video of the Chili Challenge and I need to go see it."

"Can I come with you?"

"Are you sure? It might be a long night."

"Well, I can always get an Ottermobile if it gets too late." Dani shrugged. "But I'm dying to know what Robert found."

"Okay. But no Otter. Just tell me if you need to go home and I'll drive you."

"If you insist." Dani wasn't sure why Spencer was against her using a car service, but it would only take him a few minutes to get her to the mansion and return to the campus security building, so she wouldn't feel too guilty dragging him away from the investigation.

As she started to move out of the booth, Spencer got up from his side and held out his hand. He stroked his thumb along her inner wrist and his touch stole her breath.

Spencer lifted her hand to his mouth and kissed her palm. "I do. We've been getting reports of Otter drivers assaulting their riders."

"Oh, no." Because Dani was distracted by the feeling of his lips, it took her a second respond. "We have to warn the girls!"

"I told Ivy and she promised to spread the word to your boarders." Spencer narrowed his eyes. "I assumed she'd tell you too."

"Ivy knows that I never take a service."

"That's probably it." Spencer shook his head. "We need to get word out to more of the students, but the university's legal department won't let us issue an official alert. They're afraid Ottermobile will sue us."

"Have Ivy and her friends post on social media." Dani laced my fingers with his. "No need for anything official."

"Good idea." Spencer winked. "I should have thought of that."

"The boss doesn't have to think of everything. Whoever you assign as your social media expert should automatically do things like that."

"Robert's covering the role right now," Spencer explained. "But he doesn't want it permanently."

"Maybe when you advertise for a replacement for Warren Douglas, that can be part of the job," Dani suggested.

"Another good idea." Spencer's smile was rueful. "I may have to hire you."

Dani shook her head. "I already have too many jobs."

Once the bill was paid and they were in his truck heading toward the campus security building, Dani thought about all she'd learned so far about the murder. There was something she'd wanted to ask Spencer about Warren Douglas, but no matter how hard she concentrated, she couldn't think of it.

She forced herself to quit trying to remember. Maybe if she relaxed, it would come to her as they viewed the videos that Robert had found.

Spencer parked in front of the four-story brick structure, then helped Dani out of the pickup and guided her up the sidewalk. They entered through the double glass doors and crossed the lobby to the stairway.

The security team's tactical center took up the entire top floor and when Dani and Spencer arrived, they found Robert seated at a large table with multiple monitors facing him. The rest of the room held similar stations, but there was no one currently working at any of them.

"Boss!" Robert immediately leaped to his feet and gestured to the seat he had vacated. Then noticing Dani, he quickly wheeled over a second chair for her. "Just wait till you see what I found."

"Let's do this." Spencer studied the screen in front of him.

Robert leaned over Spencer and clicked away at the keyboard. "I've been combing through various social media sites using the keyword/hashtag app and I finally found some videos recorded around the time of the propane explosion. Look at this."

"What?" Spencer leaned forward.

Dani followed suit, narrowing her eyes. She recognized the union patio. There was suddenly a closeup of one of the cooking areas. A bulky figure with his back to the camera was fiddling around with the propane tank. He straightened, checked his watch, then looked around. A baseball cap kept his face in the shadow.

Minutes ticked by and he continued to stare at his watch and scan the patio. Finally, Warren Douglas appeared at the far edge of the image.

The baseball capped figure immediately placed something near the propane tank, then took a step back. Dani saw the flare of matches, then the person leaped over the railing and ran out of view.

Meanwhile, the security guard was making his rounds, sticking his head into each cooking station as he walked through the area. A minute or two later, a ball of light filled the monitor, and the monitor went blank.

"Where did you find this?" Spencer asked.

Robert consulted a small notebook and said, "This was posted on a site called Chaos. They offer a bounty for original clips featuring death and destruction. The gorier or more heinous the better."

Dani continued to stare at the now blank monitor. She could barely grasp that she had just seen someone blown up.

Granted, all she'd really seen was a bright light, but her imagination did the rest. Her heart raced and she couldn't seem to get her lungs to expand.

Spencer faced Robert and said, "We need to find the person who shot the video."

She was glad that Spencer didn't seem to notice her distress. She'd made the decision to come here, and she didn't want him to feel guilty for her seeing the video.

Inhaling through her nose, she blew out a breath. She repeated this until she was calmer, then refocused on the conversation.

"The files are posted anonymously." Robert shook his head. "Maybe the cops can get a warrant to force the website owner to turn over the information, but we sure can't."

"Right." Spencer nodded. "We'll have to alert Detective Taylor to this video."

Dani was a little surprised he was giving up so easily.

"On the other hand," Spencer continued, "there's nothing stopping us from getting one of the computer whizzes in the university to analyze the recording and see what we can find."

Chapter 30

While Dani and Spencer grabbed sodas from the vending machine in the employee lounge, Robert went back to combing social media for any other hits. When they returned to the tactical center, the young security agent was deeply engrossed in his work.

Dani silently placed Robert's Mountain Dew near him, then she and Spencer settled in to rewatch the explosion recording frame by frame. They were hoping to find some clue as to the hooded figure's identity.

An hour later, Dani finally voiced the question that had been bothering her since seeing the footage. "How do you think whoever shot the video was able to do it without the murderer noticing?"

Spencer paused the recording and turned to Dani. "Some of the new phones can shoot from quite a distance away. There are bushes across from the patio, so the videographer could have noticed the guy messing around in the Chili Challenge cook station and hidden in the shrubs. It was no secret that someone was interfering with the competitors' stuff, so they might have even thought they could sell the footage to the company sponsoring the contest."

"So why not try to sell the recording of the explosion to UFE?"

Spencer scratched his chin. "It's one thing to expose someone committing sabotage. It's another thing to let a murderer know you were a witness."

"But he or she still wanted a payday, so they figured an anonymous website post was the safer bet." Dani paused, then asked, "But the police will eventually be able to find the person who shot the video, right?"

"Probably. However, I doubt the videographer took that into consideration. People, especially young people, feel invincible and invisible online."

Dani considered Spencer's words, then said, "So there's a good chance we're looking for a student."

"That's where I'd start."

"You know, now that we're aware of the recording, I'd say that the injured guy we helped right after the explosion was probably the videographer." Dani brightened. "Hey, didn't the ambulance take him to hospital? We could get his identity from there."

"I think he refused to be transported."

"Shoot!" Dani sighed, then she straightened and said, "I guess we'll just have to work with what we have. What can we deduce from the video?"

Spencer got up, went over to a portable

whiteboard, and pulled it over to where Dani was sitting. He picked up a dry erase marker and began to outline.

He wrote number one and spoke as he wrote. "From what Frannie and Justin told us, as well as this video, I would say Douglas was indeed the intended target."

"Which means it's extremely doubtful the explosion had anything to do with either the contest or the sponsoring company."

Nodding, Spencer put that as number two, then quickly wrote number three and said, "The conversation that Frannie and Justin relayed to us, makes it sound as if Douglas and whoever he was talking to knew each other from somewhere else."

"Yes." Dani stared at the ceiling. "And I think it's safe to assume, at least for our purposes, that the guy arguing with Douglas is also the one who killed him."

Spencer added that point to the list on the whiteboard, then asked, "Are you satisfied that the person in the video is male?"

"Hmm." Dani twirled a piece of hair around her finger. "Considering the size and shape of the figure, as well as how he moved, I would say that I'm about ninety percent sure it's a guy."

Tapping the marker against the board, Spencer said, "Or an extremely tall and husky woman.

Judging from where the person's head came up to when they straightened, I would put the murderer's height between six foot and six-two. Weight is harder to judge because they could have had several layers of clothing on."

"With Jill VanAsden and Hamilton Butcher messing around with equipment and ingredients the first day of the contest, I wonder if that's what gave the killer the idea to monkey with the propane tank. Maybe he thought the murder would be written off as a terrible accident."

Spencer grabbed his soda and took a swallow. "I agree. Is there anything else we know from either the overheard conversation or recording?"

"More like a question." Dani paused, thinking. "I've never heard of the name Boobie. Do you think it was a nickname?"

Spencer started a new column on the whiteboard headed questions. "I think that name might be the key, but in order to find out what it unlocks, we need to look into Douglas's past."

"That's it!" Dani jerked as if she'd been zapped by a cattle prod. "Where did you say Douglas worked before coming here?"

"Some hospital. Let me go grab his personnel file."

While Spencer ran down to his office, Dani

wandered over to where Robert was working. She stood at his side as he manipulated the mouse and images flittered past on the monitors.

When he came to a post featuring a video of a police department crime scene unit sitting in the union parking lot, Dani said, "Can I see that again?"

"Sure." Robert restarted the recording, and she watched as a CSI bagged the coverall Dani had found the morning of the explosion.

She bit her lip. "That reminds me of something, but what?"

"I give up." Robert chuckled.

"Me too." Dani's shoulders slumped and she went back to her seat.

As she waited for Spencer to return with the file, she closed her eyes and thought about the moments just before the propane tank blew up. *Hmm*. She'd been walking by the side of the building when Mr. Coverall had brushed past her, nearly knocking her down in his haste. A nanosecond later she'd heard and felt the boom.

It had to be the same guy as was in the video.

Dani quickly made a note to pass the information onto the police detective, then resumed her contemplation. There was something else.

Although, she hadn't recognized the person in the coverall, there was something familiar about them. They hadn't spoken, so it couldn't be the sound of their voice. What else would she have noticed?

Before she could come up with anything, Spencer appeared holding a thin manila folder. He sat next to Dani and flipped it open.

"There's not much here." Spencer rifled through the half dozen pages. "Let's start with Douglas's application. It'll have his work history."

Skimming the single sheet of paper, Dani's gaze stopped at the line for last place of employment. "Where's Thomas State Hospital?"

"Let me check." Spencer turned to the computer and tapped a few keys. "Near Bard, Arkansas."

Dani frowned. "There's no one I can think associated with the Chili Challenge from Arkansas."

"True." Spencer narrowed his eyes. "But there were contestants from Kansas, Missouri, and Oklahoma, which are all states that are close to Arkansas."

"Too bad Jill, Elvis, and Milton have returned home." Dani blew out a frustrated breath.

"They haven't left yet. The police chief told me they asked the contestants to stick around for a couple more days."

"And they agreed?"

"Let's just say Detective Taylor made it clear that whoever left would become his prime suspect."

Chapter 31

"Good news." Spencer's voice crackled with satisfaction as it came through the speaker on Dani's cell phone. "The police were able to clear all the judges and media, which leaves only the contestants."

"Or some rando who wandered onto the campus," Dani muttered.

She was cranky after preparing the Lunch-to-Go meals by herself. Her scheduled helper, Starr, was down with a cold and none of the other girls had been available.

Spencer chuckled. "Did you get out of the wrong side of the bed?"

"All the sides are the wrong ones when all you want to do is sleep in."

Dani yawned. She was exhausted after her late night with Spencer at the campus security office. One of these days, she needed to put some time aside and sleep twenty-four hours straight.

"Maybe you can take a nap later," Spencer soothed. "Anyway, the chief has greenlighted our talking to Jill, Elvis, and Milton."

Dani yawned again. "When?"

"Are you free now?"

Dani looked around her kitchen. "Yes. But give me an hour to clean up my prep area, shower, and change clothes."

"Okay, then I'll pick you up about two."

Placing a large bowl in the dishwasher, Dani asked, "Where are we going?"

"The police are putting up the remaining contestants at the Regency Park Suites. Jennalynn Mires, one of my former employees, is head of security there, and she's arranging for us to use an office for the interviews."

Dani wiped down the counter. "Do the suspects know we're coming?"

"Not exactly. I left them all messages that they would be briefed on the case's progress today and asked that they make themselves available this afternoon." Spencer cleared his throat. "I may have led them to believe that the message was from the police."

The front doorbell rang, and Dani hurriedly said her goodbyes. The head honcho from her dad's company was right on time. Now if only he'd agree to her compromise.

* * *

When Jill VanAsden entered the office that Dani and Spencer were using at the Regency Park, Dani was taken aback at the woman's appearance. Instead of the confident soccer mom from the cooking contest, Jill looked as if she hadn't slept in a week or bothered to shower either.

Jill wore sweatpants and a stained T-shirt. Her hair was scraped into a greasy ponytail, and smudged glasses adorned her makeup-free face. Gone were the sleek bob, contact lenses, and designer athleisurewear.

Spencer sat behind a sleek chrome and glass desk and Dani occupied one of the two leather and chrome chairs facing him. Jill shot her a puzzled look as she took the vacant seat but remained silent.

Spencer opened a folder on the desktop and said, "Ms. VanAsden, I appreciate you agreeing to see us."

"As if I had a choice," Jill muttered, then blinked. "Hey, you're the security guy from the college, I thought I was coming here to talk to the police."

Spencer's expression remained impassive. "The police have approved this meeting and we won't take up much of your time."

"Fine." Jill shrugged. "It beats watching daytime TV."

Spencer flipped through the file. "I see you're from Kansas. Are you familiar with the town of Bard, Arkansas?"

"I don't think so. I'm from Northwest Kansas. We're nowhere near Arkansas."

Frowning, Spencer rifled through the papers in front of him. "And you haven't had any reason to travel to Bard, maybe visited someone there?"

"No." Jill blew out an exasperated breath. "I'm a stay-at-home mom and before this trip, the only traveling I've done in years was for my son's soccer games." She held up her hand. "Before you ask, his team has never played in Arkansas."

Spencer wrote something down, then said, "I'm aware that you've worked things out with the police regarding your gun issue. But have you had any contact with the Chili Challenge people about switching Tory Mays's ingredients?"

"Of course not. It was just a joke." Jill fingered a small tear in her sweatpants. "Tory substituted sugar for my salt, but I didn't have a camera aimed at my area so I can't prove it."

Spencer raised a brow, then said, "I suppose since neither of you came in first, second, or third, and thus didn't win any prize money, there's no harm, no foul."

"That's right." Jill glared at Dani. "You all should be looking at the winners, not the rest of us."

Spencer nodded. "Maybe. But you, Milton, and Elvis are the three contestants who didn't provide an alibi to the police."

"How about her?" Jill pointed at Dani.

Chuckling, Spencer said, "She has the best alibi of all. She was with me during the time frame."

"How do you know the time frame?" Jill demanded, plainly frustrated that Dani was in the clear.

Spencer explained, "Well, the police already had a pretty good idea, but we've located a video of the incident so now they have an exact moment the propane tank was sabotaged."

Jill's expression brightened. "If you have a recording, then you know who did it."

Spencer shot Dani a glance, then said, "Not yet, but as soon as the techies finish with it, we will. So now is the time to come clean and make a deal with the police before they don't have to offer you one."

"I told that stupid detective, and I'll tell you. I didn't do it." Jill's eyes were glossy, and a tear slipped down her cheek. "I sure wish I hadn't decided to sleep in that day. No one believes my husband, and he's the only one that saw me before we went down to the cooking area."

Dani wrinkled her brow. Why didn't that sound right? As Spencer continued to question Jill, Dani tuned them out and concentrated.

Finally, she remembered.

Choosing her words carefully, she turned to Jill and asked, "Wait a minute, Elvis mentioned seeing you and your husband at the Pancake House that morning just prior to the explosion."

"He must have been mistaken. Like I said, my husband and I slept in." Jill frowned. "We just used the hotel coffee maker and ate the protein bars from our welcome basket."

Spencer met Dani's eye and shot her a questioning look, then quickly stood, and said, "Thank you for talking to us, Ms. VanAsden. I'm sure the police will be in touch soon."

Jill slowly rose from her chair and moved to where Spencer was holding open the door, but before she stepped out of the office, she said, "I really had nothing to do with that explosion. When do you think the cops will let me go home?"

"I wish I could say." Spencer patted her shoulder.

"My son needs me." Jill looked back as she walked away. "My husband went home to him, but Jay's only eight and I've never been away from him this long before."

Dani's heart went out to the woman. She wished she could reassure her that it would be over soon.

"Did Elvis really say he saw the VanAsdens at breakfast on Saturday?" Spencer dropped into the chair next to Dani and rubbed his temples.

Dani nodded. "I forgot to tell you or Gray that at

the dinner on Sunday, Elvis claimed to have seen Jill and her husband at the Pancake House Saturday morning right before the explosion."

"You would think that Elvis would have told Christensen or Taylor himself when he was asked for an alibi."

"Maybe he realized he'd been mistaken about the day he saw them," Dani suggested.

"Possibly." Spencer pursed his lips. "But he is the contestant who's the most similar in size to the person in the video. Milton is tall enough, but he'd have had to been wearing a lot of clothes to look that bulky. And Jill is just too short, although her husband is tall enough."

Dani sighed. She'd thought of that. But hoped there was some other explanation. She'd liked Elvis and hated to think of him as a killer.

Chapter 32

Dani and Spencer's next interview was with Milton McBeal, the attorney from Oklahoma. The conversation was short, but not sweet. He'd immediately informed them that he'd invoked his right to remain silent with the police and he certainly wasn't changing his mind and talking to some rent-a-cop and his girlfriend.

With that statement, he got to his feet and stomped out of the office. He paused at the door and announced that he'd already started the wheels turning on lawsuits against the Normalton police department, the Normalton University, and USA Foodservice Equipment.

Once Milton had disappeared, Dani blew a strand of hair out of her eyes and scoffed. "That went well."

"Yeah, but although I'd really like that jerk to be the murderer," Spencer rolled his eyes, "I seriously doubt that he'd have the balls to do it."

Dani tapped the arm of her chair. "Absolutely. Messing around with a propane tank and fire takes more *cajónes* than Mr. I'm-an-Important-Lawyer strikes me as having in his jeans. He'd be much more likely to slap someone with an injunction than actually hit them."

Spencer nodded his agreement, then picked up the desk telephone. "I'll call Elvis's room and tell him we're ready to talk to him."

Dani watched as Spencer dialed. She could hear the phone ringing and ringing. After the seventh ring, Spencer frowned and placed the receiver in the cradle.

He immediately tried again, but when he got the same result, he hung up and said, "That's odd. The three contestants were all told to remain in their room until they were summoned to this office."

"Could he be in the bathroom?" Dani thought about the possibilities. "Or maybe his room has a balcony and he's sitting out there?"

Spencer stroked his chin. "You have his cell number from when he texted you, right?"

"I should." Dani took her phone out of her purse and scrolled through her messages looking for the one from Elvis. It took a while, but she finally found it and asked, "Shall I call him?"

"Sure."

Dani tapped the screen and heard two rings, then an automated voice announced, "This number is no longer in service."

"That's odd." Dani stared at her cell as if it might

give her an explanation.

Spencer picked up the desk phone. "I'll try his room one more time."

"I hope he's okay," Dani worried. "Maybe we're wrong about Warren Douglas being the intended target. The killer might have been after Elvis all along."

Spencer hesitated, then said, "I suppose, but I don't think so."

When no one answered Spencer's call, he stood. You stay here in case Elvis shows up, and I'll get Jennalynn's key and check his room."

While she waited for Spencer, Dani looked at her messages. There were two business calls, one asking if she was free to cater a wedding brunch and another inquiring about her services as a personal chef.

Dani returned both calls, answered the perspective clients' questions, and entered the information on her scheduling spreadsheet app. When she finished, she noticed that Spencer had been gone nearly forty-five minutes. What was taking him so long?

She got to her feet and walked to the office door. The hallway was empty, and she wasn't sure what to do next. Should she call him?

No. It might have taken Spencer a while to find Jennalynn and get her passkey. Dani would give him fifteen more minutes, then text him.

She used the time to look up Thomas State Hospital. She'd been meaning to research Warren Douglas' previous employer and hadn't got around to it. Maybe there was a clue about his past in the place he'd worked prior to joining Normalton University's security team.

Dani navigated to the hospital's website and read: THOMAS STATE HOSPITAL IS AMONG THE OLDEST PUBLIC MENTAL HEALTH FACILITIES IN THE MIDWEST. IT IS ALSO ONE OF THE MOST HIGHLY ENDORSED FACILITIES WEST OF THE MISSISSIPPI RIVER FOR CIVIL INVOLUNTARY DETENTIONS.

Wow! She hadn't been expecting that.

Resting her head on the back of the chair, Dani stared at the ceiling. Was that the piece of the puzzle they'd been missing?

Her eyes drifted shut and she had nearly dozed off when someone grabbed her by the shoulders. She shrieked and tried to stand, but Elvis Larson loomed over her, a scowl on his usually good-natured face.

Dani quickly ran through various scenarios and decided that if was best to try to act normally. "Uh, hi, Elvis, we, um, were just waiting for you. Spencer went looking for you. Did you see him?"

"Shut up!" His fingers dug into the flesh of her

upper arm pressing her back into her seat. "Your boyfriend won't be coming to your rescue."

"Oh. Did he get distracted by a call from the college?" Dani's laugh was forced. "That happens a lot, I should probably be mad."

"Drop the act. Jill came to me and demanded to know why I had said I'd seen her at the pancake restaurant. I told her that I just made a mistake and we chatted for a while. When she told me you guys had a video, I knew it was only a matter of time before you figured out it was me."

Had Elvis really just confessed?

Dani fought to keep her face expressionless. "So why didn't you just get out of here and disappear?" She slipped her free hand into her purse and grasped the small can of pepper spray attached to her keyring.

"I was going to do that, but you guys didn't take as long with McBeal as I thought you would, and as I was leaving my room, I saw Drake getting out of the elevator." Elvis sighed. "I figured he was already suspicious of me, first the alibi that turned out to be a fake one—I was really hoping you didn't remember me saying that—then me not answering my phone. Which is why you need to come with me as my get-out-of-jail-free card. Once I'm sure that I'm not being followed, I'll let you out at a rest area or gas station."

Dani's heart pounding, she swallowed hard.

"What did you do to Spencer?"

"He's somewhere he can't come after me. He's not dead, but..." Elvis hesitated, staring over her shoulder unwilling to meet her gaze. "The faster we get away and you're able to come back and search for him, the better."

This was her chance. Elvis was distracted.

Dani jerked free from the big man's grip and emptied the pepper spray directly into his eyes.

He howled, clawing at his face.

Dani dashed down the empty hallway frantically looking for help. She could hear Elvis yelling, then his footsteps thundering after her.

She quickly pressed the elevator button, but when the doors didn't immediately open, she headed for the staircase.   A second after she made it onto the landing, the doorknob rattled, and Dani only had a nanosecond to decide what to do.

She quickly slipped behind the door, and when Elvis pushed it open, she had to swallow the pain of it slamming into her body without making a sound. He paused, looking around, then headed to the steps. As he leaned over and peered down the stairs, Dani darted forward and shoved him with all her strength.

At first, he teetered, nearly regaining his balance, but one more thrust from her and he fell.

Without waiting to see how far he tumbled

down, she whirled around and ran back into the corridor, praying the elevator had arrived.

Chapter 33

Dani came to a dead stop staring at the lighted panel above the elevators. The hotel had fourteen floors. The convention staff offices were on the seventh, and a thirteen was illuminated over one set of doors and a twelve over the others. Should she wait?

She anxiously scanned the hallway. The only way out seemed to be either the steps that she'd pushed Elvis down or the elevators. And she definitely wasn't going back to the staircase.

Dani glanced at all the closed doors along the corridor. Jennalynn had explained that the convention staff were away today at a meeting at the national headquarters, and that Dani and Spencer had the floor to themselves.

She'd left her purse and cell phone in the office they'd been using for the interviews. Maybe she could lock herself in there and phone for help.

No! If Elvis had survived the fall down the steps and wasn't too badly injured, that was the first place he would look for her. Her only hope was to get into one of the other offices and use a landline.

Checking the elevators one more time, she saw

that neither car had budged. She couldn't wait any longer. She needed to get someone looking for Spencer.

Dani started up the hall, trying each door as she came to it. They were all locked, and she kept looking over her shoulder, half expecting to see Elvis charging toward her.

As she worked her way down the corridor, her mind kept coming back to why Elvis would have murdered Warren Douglas. The grill master had seemed like such a nice guy. What would cause him to snap like that?

It had to have something to do with the security guard's past employment. Had Elvis had a loved one in that hospital? Or had he been involuntarily committed there himself?

Dani hadn't had any luck finding an open door so when she reached the office they'd been using, she decided to duck in, grab her phone and purse, then get right out again.

Her heart pounding, she grasped the knob and pulled, but stumbled forward when the door remained firmly closed. Elvis must have locked it when he took off after her.

Shit! Now what?

Suddenly, she heard the elevator ping.

Pivoting on her heel, she turned and ran. Praying

she'd get there in time, she sprinted back down the hallway and threw herself at the closing doors.

Dani managed to shove them open and stumbled inside. Turning toward the indicator panel on the wall, Dani screamed in frustration.

The reason it had taken the elevator so long to arrive was that someone had pushed all the buttons. It would stop on every floor on the way down, and Elvis could be on any one of those waiting for her.

A tear slipped down Dani's cheek. How would she save Spencer, not to mention herself?

Pulling herself together, Dani immediately engaged the emergency stop. Now that there was no danger of the door opening to an enraged Elvis, she examined the rest of the options on the panel.

A button with a picture of a receiver caught her gaze. Pushing it, she waited for someone to answer.

"What is your emergency?"

The soothing female voice did wonders to calm Dani, and she explained her situation. Silence greeted her story.

It was evident that the operator didn't immediately believe Dani, but after a few minutes, she said, "I've called the police. They are sending officers. The elevator will remain stopped until they are in position at the sixth floor."

"How about Chief Drake? Is anyone looking for

him?" Dani demanded.

"The police have asked us to wait for their arrival."

Dani's head throbbed, her temper threatening to get the best of her. "And Elvis?" Is anyone checking the staircase?"

"The police —"

"Let me guess, no search until they get here."

If she hadn't killed him by shoving him down the steps, he could be halfway to Missouri by now. Or headed back to wherever he'd stashed Spencer to use him as a hostage. They had to do something now!

The voice from the speaker broke into Dani's spiraling thoughts. "The elevator will begin descending in a few seconds. When the door opens, raise your hands in the air, and wait for instructions."

"What?" Dani squeaked.

Why did she need to raise her hands? She was the victim here.

The voice intoned, "Remain calm."

Before Dani could respond, the door slid open and a female officer yelled, "Hands up!"

Dani immediately complied, then said, "You need to find Chief Drake. Elvis said he was okay for now, but who knows how long that will remain true."

"Slowly come out of the elevator." The woman ignored Dani. "Do you have any weapons?"

Dani scowled. "Of course not. Why are you treating me like this?"

"Mr. Larson was found at the bottom of the stairwell, severely injured and he claims that you snuck up on him and pushed him."

Tears welled up in Dani's eyes. "It was self-defense. He'd already admitted to locking away Chief Drake and was attempting to take me as a hostage."

"Be that as it may," the police officer shrugged, "you're coming with me down to the station and we'll sort it all out there."

"But—"

"If you don't cooperate, I'll cuff you and take you in that way."

Dani shook her head. "No. I'm happy to go with you, but how about Chief Drake?"

"We have a pair of officers searching floor to floor for him. They've started at ground level and are working their way up." The officer motioned for Dani to step back into the elevator. "Now let's go."

Just as Dani started to comply, a familiar voice rang out, "Stand down, Officer Marman. You were told to rescue Ms. Sloan, not arrest her."

"Gray!" Dani rushed past the officer toward her friend. "Have they found Spencer?"

"Not yet. But we will." Gray Christensen examined Dani and asked, "Are you alright?"

"Yes. A bit shaken up, but physically fine."

"Good." Gray directed his attention to the woman standing by the elevator glowering. "Officer Marman, I'm going to give you the benefit of the doubt and assume that you misheard your orders. Now report to the first floor and help the others look for Chief Drake."

"Yes, sir." The young woman shot Dani an angry look, retreated into the elevator.

Dani gestured toward the closing metal doors. "What was that all about?"

Gray blew out a frustrated breath. "Trista wants to make detective. And she's convinced herself that if she figures out something that the lead on the case has missed, that's her ticket to a golden shield."

"But you do have Elvis in custody, right?"

Gray sighed. "Not at this moment. We found him trying to get out of the stairwell exit and called for an ambulance. He did make that ridiculous claim against you, but no one believed him."

"Except Trista," Dani teased.

"Right." Gray didn't smile, instead he rubbed his neck and said, "Unfortunately, Larson convinced the paramedic that he was more severely injured than he really was and when the guy turned his back, Larson knocked him out and escaped as soon as the ambulance stopped for traffic."

Dani's chest tightened in fear. "So, he's on the loose?"

Gray patted her arm. "We'll find him. He may not have been as badly hurt as he claimed, but he was definitely not moving very fast."

"Can we join the search for Spencer?" Dani asked, trying to forget about what Elvis could be doing on the loose.

"I don't suppose you'd be willing to wait for me in the lobby?"

"Absolutely not." Dani sucked in her breath, feeling the pain and terror Spencer might be experiencing. "What if he's injured and time is of the essence? The more eyes the better."

"Any idea where we should look?"

"Actually, I do."

Chapter 34

After Dani explained her idea to Gray, he said, "Okay, Elvis's room was on the twelfth floor, let's head up there and see if you're right."

The elevator ride was silent and when the door slid open, Dani rushed out. Gray followed her and they headed toward 1205.

Dani examined the area. "Elvis said that Spencer arrived just as he was leaving, so he concealed himself and was then able to sneak up on Spencer and overcome him. Elvis would have had to stash Spencer fairly close to his room, otherwise, he risked being seen by a fellow hotel guest."

"I agree." Spencer ducked into an open area a few steps down the hall and said, "Let's see what's in here."

Dani joined him. The alcove held a soda machine and an ice maker.

She walked over to look behind both and spotted a twenty-by-twenty-inch door flush with the wall. There was no knob, and she couldn't see a way to open it.

Running her fingers over the surface, she felt a small slot. "I think this takes a key."

"Let me see." Gray nudged her gently out of the way.

Dani took a step back. "If it takes a key, Elvis wouldn't have been able to get in."

"This is a service hatch, probably so workers can access plumbing or electrical conduit." Gray reached into his pocket and pulled out a Swiss Army knife. "A flathead screwdriver should open it."

Dani held her breath as Gray eased the door open. At first, all she could see was pipes running every which way, but then she made out a slumped figure and nearly pushed Gray over in her frenzy to get closer.

"Hold on." Gray eased into the tiny space and Dani could hear moaning as he backed out dragging Spencer's limp body after him.

Dani rushed forward, her heart pounding in her ears. "Is he okay?"

Gray ignored her question, laid Spencer on the floor, and handed Dani his phone. "Call for an ambulance." He examined Spencer as Dani tapped 911.

Just as Dani reached the dispatcher and ask for help, Spencer stirred and tried to sit up.

"Whoa." Gray pressed him down. "Rest. We're getting you help."

Spencer propped himself against the soda

machine and asked, "What happened?"

"We think Elvis conked you on the back of the head and stuffed you in a service hatch," Gray answered.

"Did he get away?"

Before Gray could answer, Dani heard the sound of footsteps thundering towards them and Elvis rushed around the corner. His maniacal grin reminded her of Jack Nicholson in *The Shining*, except that instead of brandishing an ax, he was wielding an IV pole in one hand and gun in the other.

Dani slipped the phone into her pocket. The dispatcher was still on the line, and she hoped the woman could hear what was going on.

Gray held up both hands and said, "Put the weapons down, Mr. Larson. We can work something out where no one gets hurt."

Elvis sneered. "You two," he pointed at the men, "get back in that service hatch. Ms. Nosey here is driving me to Missouri."

Spencer wobbled to his feet and ducked around Dani and Gray. He stuck his hand in his pockets and dangled his keys. "Here. We can take my truck. I'll drive you. You don't need Dani."

Lumbering forward, Elvis put the gun to Spencer's forehead and said, "She owes me."

Dani gulped. She had to go with him. He was

just too volatile. Elvis might kill Spencer if he kept
trying to protect her.

Her mind raced as he herded Gray and Spencer
into the service hatch. Could she stall until the
paramedics arrived?

Raising her voice so she could be heard through
the open line on the phone in her pocket, she said,
"I'll go with you, but why did you want Warren
Douglas dead?"

"I didn't." Elvis let go of the IV pole and pushed
Spencer into the opening. "But he was going to ruin
everything."

"You knew him from Thomas State Hospital,
didn't you?" Dani continued to speak loudly.

"Yeah," Elvis shoved Gray in after Spencer. "He
was a security guard there when the court put my
mother in that hellhole."

Dani hadn't been expecting that answer, and it
took her a second to process the information, but then
she said, "And Mr. Douglas was trying to blackmail
you over that?"

"Not exactly that. Something else." Elvis
replaced the door to the hatch and motioned for Dani
to start walking.

"What?" Dani moved as slowly as possible,
shocked Elvis was telling her any of this and deep
down she was afraid that his openness meant he

would kill her after her usefulness as a hostage was over.

Elvis put the gun against her back and urged her forward, his southern accent increasing as he explained, "Momma was in the hospital 'cause she saw stuff that wasn't there and heard voices tellin' her that Daddy was an alien tryin' to kill her."

"Oh?" Dani's heart broke for Elvis, but she continued to drag her feet. "It must've been tough seeing your mom that way."

Elvis gulped, then as he continued to drive her toward the elevator, he said, "It was when Momma tried to gas Daddy with carbon monoxide, that the courts put her in Thomas."

"Okay." Dani stopped, stalling for time. "I still don't understand what Douglas was holding over you."

Elvis seized her arm and dragged her in front of the buttons, pushing the DOWN one. "Of course, you don't."

"Then explain it to me."

The elevator doors opened, and Elvis tightened his hold on Dani's arm and hauled her inside, shoving her to the back of the car. "Because Momma was what they termed delusional, when she told the hospital people that the doctor had been molesting her no one believed her."

"But you did."

Elvis nodded, pushed the button for the underground garage, then when the doors closed, he let go of Dani's arm. "And I took care of that doctor."

"Took care of…?" Dani leaned against the wall, rubbing her bicep, and watched the lighted buttons above the door blink downward to her doom.

"Douglas saw me beating the crap out of him and that scumbag security guard demanded five thousand dollars to say the doctor was mistaken and it wasn't me who thumped him."

"And when Douglas spotted you here, he decided it was time for another payoff?"

"Yep. After nearly hitting me with his car Friday after lunch, he threw a note on the ground with instructions on how I was to pay him another five thousand. It was still an open case so he could have suddenly *remembered* seeing me there."

Before Dani could reply, the elevator door slid open. Several police officers stood with their guns drawn, and Dani immediately hit the floor to get out of any possible line of fire.

Elvis tried to grab her, but the cops had the drop on him, and he had no choice but to give up his weapon.

While they dragged him out of the elevator and secured him, Dani remained on the floor. Once he was handcuffed, she rose and rushed toward the nearest officer.

It was the woman who had tried to arrest her, but Dani ignored that and said, "You need to send help to the twelfth floor. Detective Christensen and Chief Drake are locked in a service hatch."

"Actually," the woman gestured behind her, "they're not. And your boyfriend refused to go to the hospital until you were safe."

Spencer limped forward and swept Dani in his arms. "Now we can both go and get checked out."

Epilogue

A few months ago, Dani had started a new tradition at the mansion. Since she rarely had catering or private chef gigs on Sunday evenings, all her tenants and their significant others gathered in the family room for pizza and games.

It was a way to encourage a more family-like feeling among the renters and for Dani to check in on everyone at the end of the week. Spencer insisted that Sunday was the beginning of a new week, and he was technically correct, but to Dani, Monday always felt like it should hold that title.

Tonight, five days after Elvis had been charged with the murder of Warren Douglas, everyone was sprawled on various pieces of furniture or on cushions and beanbags brought down from the second-floor bedrooms.

Udell Williams was a new addition, invited by Atti as a thank you for helping her with her pervy professor. He had only returned to Normalton a few hours earlier after a trip to Chicago where he'd helped his mom's congregation put a new roof on the church.

Dani had been a bit surprised to see him, but

happy that he and Atti had hit it off so well. She had briefly wondered if she should have asked Jonas to join them. Maybe next time she'd include her father.

The individual pizza pot pies that Dani and the girls had concocted had been a big hit, and the men had just finished cleaning up the kitchen. Now everyone was trying to overcome their digestive stupor and choose a game.

After having spent so much time enmeshed in the greed and misery of the chili contest and then the murder, this get-together was exactly what Dani needed.

Dani smiled as Ivy and Justin argued for a trivia game, they both had super high IQs and enjoyed a challenge. The others just wanted to relax and play something more lighthearted.

Okay with either choice, Dani looked at Spencer, who was sitting next to her on the couch, and asked, "Have you heard anything about the case against Elvis?"

She'd seen him admitted to the hospital while she and Spencer were there being checked out for injuries. And the last she knew he was still there under guard.

"His lawyer is using every stall tactic in the book," Spencer answered, wincing as he grabbed his bottle of water from the end table.

"Are you okay, Uncle Spencer?" Ivy leaned around her boyfriend, Laz, who was sharing her bean bag, and wrinkled her brow. "Is it your bruised ribs?"

Spencer smiled at his niece. "I'm fine. They're getting better every day."

"How about your head?" Ivy twirled a strand of her long blonde hair and frowned. "You were lucky that awful man didn't give you a concussion."

"The tenderness is nearly gone."

"What kind of stall tactics is the attorney using?" Frannie asked from her spot on the club chair. "The guy confessed in front of three witnesses, one of whom was a police officer, and dispatcher heard him over the phone."

"The lawyer's claiming that Elvis was dazed after Dani pushed him down the stairs." Spencer scowled. "Fortunately, the hotel security cameras caught him chasing her in the hallway, so there's no way that his story that she attacked him first will hold up."

"Yeah," Atti lay on the carpet, leaning back on her elbows, "that was real fortunate. You know what would have been better? If you didn't put her in danger."

"Seriously?" Tippi walked into the family room from the kitchen and sat next to her boyfriend, Caleb. "Dani is her own person. Nobody allows her to do something. She's not a child."

Hastily changing the subject, Dani turned to Justin, who was seated near his fiancée on her chair's matching ottoman. "Did the paper ever figure out who sent the threatening emails?"

"Yeah. It was that vegan guy."

Spencer snorted. "Big surprise. Hamilton Butcher admitted that when he couldn't sabotage Dani's workstation because Atti scared him off, he set the dumpster fire behind the mansion. He wanted to save animals but was willing to put people at risk. What a jerk."

"Absolutely." Dani nodded, then frowned. "Hey, did you or the police ever find out who Ruben was arguing with and what that quarrel was about?"

Spencer chuckled. "I spoke with him, and it turned out, he didn't even know the guy. It was just someone who he struck up a conversation with about football. The guy evidently started talking trash about the Phoenix Cardinals loss to the Kansas City Chiefs."

Everyone laughed, then Starr scooted forward on the loveseat she was sharing with her boyfriend, Robert, and said, "I know at first you said you didn't want to talk about it, Dani, but can you guys tell us how Elvis came to kill Warren Douglas?"

"Yeah." Udell had claimed the recliner and considering his size no one had challenged him for the comfy seat. "We're dying to hear what happened."

Dani and Spencer exchanged a look, and Spencer nodded toward Frannie and Justin. "Douglas was overheard saying that the person we now know was Elvis had better make it worthwhile for him to keep his mouth shut or he'd let everyone know what Elvis really was."

"So, he was blackmailing Elvis?" Caleb frowned. "About what?"

Dani took over. "Elvis's mom was hospitalized for a mental illness, and while she was being treated, her psychiatrist sexually abused her. The administration didn't believe her, so Elvis took the matter into his own hands. He snuck up on the doctor, put a bag over his head, and beat the crap out of him. Douglas witnessed it, but, for a price, testified it wasn't Elvis. When the two men ran into each other again, he demanded more money. Then when Elvis tried to leave town, Douglas phoned him and said he wasn't getting away that easily. So, Elvis returned to Normalton and set up the propane explosion."

"As we saw from the video that Robert found," Spencer took a swig of water, "Elvis opened the tank's valve, then waited for Douglas to start his rounds. Once the man was nearby, Elvis put a book of lit matches next to the propane tank and ran away."

"Elvis was the guy in the coverall that ran into me," Dani explained. "And the injured guy who came around the corner next was the videographer."

"The police found the guy who made the recording?" Caleb asked.

Robert nodded. "Once they were able to get a warrant for the website, it was a piece of cake."

"I still don't understand why Douglas called Elvis Boobie." Frannie narrowed her eyes. "Was he insulting him by calling him an idiot?"

"Nope." Atti grinned. "Clearly, none of you are fans of the king. Elvis Presley's mom called him Boobie, and I bet Douglas heard our Elvis's mother calling her son that too."

Spencer scowled. "That didn't come up when I googled Boobie."

"For me either." Justin shook his head, then shrugged. "Now that we have everything about the murder explained, can we play our game?"

Everyone agreed, and they spent the rest of the evening enmeshed in Cards Against Humanity. By the time they finished the game, Dani was yawning.

Slowly everyone drifted away, leaving Dani and Spencer in the kitchen as she did one final wipe down of the counters. She stared at the granite. There was something she needed to tell Spencer, what?

Dani mentally snapped her fingers. Her deal

with the UFE CEO. She had to come clean about it.

"Hey, now that we're alone, do you want a Corona?" Dani maintained a strict no-alcohol policy for her boarders but kept a secret stash of beer and wine for the adults.

Spencer looked surprised. "I was thinking of leaving so you could get some sleep, but I'd love a beer."

After fetching Spencer's Corona and pouring herself a glass of wine, Dani slid onto the stool next to Spencer. They each took a long sip, then both started to speak at once.

"I was only going to say that I was glad this case was solved." Spencer tipped his head toward Dani. "What did you want to talk about?"

Dani licked her lips. "Did I tell you that the CEO of UFE came over here the other day?"

"Zorillo?"

Dani shook her head. "He's the president. This was his boss, Victor Josephson."

"What did he want?"

Dani took a deep breath and explained Josephson's demand, then said, "Since I didn't want to go behind your back or get my dad fired, I proposed a compromise."

"Which was?"

Dani couldn't tell how Spencer was taking the

news and her chest tightened. "I said that I would give him a heads-up if we discovered that the murder had anything to do with his company."

"And it didn't, so that's that, right?"

Dani grimaced. "Sort of. I also said that if we found out who the killer was, once he'd been caught and turned over to the police, Josephson would be the first to know."

"Did you tell him about Elvis?"

"I texted him from the hospital. I was afraid his police informant would get to him first and he'd decide that I had broken our agreement and fire my father." Dani studied the ripples in her Moscato. "Afterwards, I realized that I should have talked to you about that first." She looked up at him through her eyelashes. "Are you upset with me?"

Spencer didn't answer right away, and Dani's pulse raced. What if he was really mad?

Finally, he said, "I do wish you had talked to me about this. But with how quickly everything happened, I can understand why you did what you did." He took her hands and stared into her eyes. "But and this is a big but, you know that after what I went through with my ex-wife, I won't tolerate being lied to or having you keep secrets from me."

Dani nodded, her throat too dry to speak.

"Just promise me that no matter what, we'll

always be honest with each other."

"I promise." Dani squeezed his fingers, then chuckled. "I always tell the girls that if you tell the truth, then you don't have to remember so much."

"Then, here's to a bad memory." Spencer lifted his bottle and Dani clinked her glass against it.

THE END

Thank you for reading Chili Chili Bang Bang. I'm thrilled you chose to spend your time with my characters and I hope you enjoyed their story.

Reviews help other readers find the books they want to read. So before you go, please leave a review, tweet, share or recommend it to your friends.

Join me on Facebook [http://www.facebook.com/DeniseSwansonAuthor] or visit my website [http://www.DeniseSwanson.com] or follow me on Twitter [DeniseSwansonAu].

Subscribe to the Denise Swanson e-newsletter for quarterly or semi-annual updates about her books and events, plus occasional recipes and other news!

Write to Denise at **ScumbleRiver@aol.com** with **Subscribe** in the Subject line and your own **E-Mail Address, First Name** and **Last Name** in the Body:

Send To: ScumbleRiver@aol.com

Subject: Subscribe

E-Mail Address:
First Name:
Last Name:

ABOUT THE AUTHOR

New York Times Bestseller author Denise Swanson was a practicing school psychologist for twenty-two years. Chili Chili Bang Bang is the fourth in Denise Swanson's Chef-to-Go mystery series. She also writes the Scumble River and Devereaux's Dime Store mysteries, the Forever Charmed paranormal mystery series, and the Change of Heart and Delicious contemporary romance series.

Denise's books have been finalists for the Agatha, Mary Higgins Clark, RT Magazine's Career Achievement, and Daphne du Maurier Awards. She has won the Reviewers Choice Award and was a BookSense 76 Top Pick.

Denise Swanson lives in Illinois with her husband, classical composer David Stybr.

For more information, please check her website http://www.DeniseSwanson.com or find Denise on Facebook at http://www.facebook.com/DeniseSwansonAuthor or follow her on Twitter at DeniseSwansonAu

Made in the USA
Las Vegas, NV
01 October 2023

78431091R00149